A PUZZLE IN
PAXTON PARK

A PAXTON PARK MYSTERY BOOK 3

J. A. WHITING

To hear about new books and book sales, please sign up for my mailing list at:

www.jawhiting.com

❀ Created with Vellum

For my family with love

1

In the waning early evening October light, twenty-eight-year-old Shelly Taylor and her friend and neighbor, Juliet Landers, stuffed an old shirt full of leaves and tied off the bottom and the ends of the sleeves with twine. Carrying the torso to the front porch, they secured it to the pair of jeans that were propped in a chair and already filled with dry leaves. Shelly pushed a pole through the shirt's neck hole and Juliet placed a pumpkin onto the pole with care.

"There. The head's on." Juliet stepped back to admire the pumpkin-headed scarecrow they'd created. "It looks great. That face you drew on the pumpkin is perfect."

"I didn't want it to look too scary," Shelly said.

"There will be a lot of little kids trick-or-treating and I don't want them to be afraid to come up on the porch and ring the bell."

Shelly's Calico cat, Justice, cautiously approached the strange thing sitting in the porch rocking chair and stretched out her neck to sniff one of the legs. Standing on her back legs and with the muscles of her body tense, the cat sniffed part of the scarecrow's arm.

"It's okay, Justice," Shelly told the feline with a chuckle. "It's only a Halloween decoration."

Satisfied that the odd creation would probably do her no harm, Justice padded away and jumped up on the porch railing where she could sit and watch the goings-on in the quiet neighborhood. Shelly and Juliet's bungalow cottages sat side by side on the lane that ran off of Main Street in the mountain resort town of Paxton Park.

Stores, restaurants, pubs, coffee shops, a movie theatre, bed and breakfast inns, and a corner market lined the brick walkways that led to the town center and a wide, green common with an old-fashioned bandstand. No matter the season, Paxton Park drew tourists and visitors throughout the year and autumn was always a busy time with people coming to the mountains to view the colorful foliage.

Pumpkins and yellow mums decorated the porch steps leading into Shelly's rented bungalow, and cornstalks were tied with orange ribbons to the sides of the porch rails.

"We should make a scarecrow to enter in the town contest." Juliet took a seat in one of the porch rocking chairs.

"We missed the deadline," Shelly pointed out. "Anyway, have you seen the entries? They're terrific."

"Let's walk by the common to take a look at them before we go to the movie," Juliet suggested. "We can get some inspiration for next year."

"We need to plan the menu for the night before Halloween," Shelly said. "The fall festival weekend is going to come fast."

Shelly and Juliet had planned a dinner for their friends to gather and eat together before they headed to the town festival for the music, bonfire, and fireworks. A long table would be set outside in the backyard under Juliet's arbor for drinks and appetizers. Torches would ring the yard, lanterns would be set along the walkway, and little orange lights were going to be strung over the branches of the big tree. Everyone would go to Shelly's house for the buffet dinner, and then the group would stroll into town for the festivities.

A town Realtor drove past the house and she waved at Shelly and Juliet as she passed by.

Juliet said, "Nora's house is getting a lot of interest. I bet it will sell quickly."

Seventy-something Nora Blake previously lived at the end of the road in a house she'd owned for forty years. Her son, Paul, had been arrested not long ago for the murder of a town teenager and shortly afterwards, Nora packed up, put her place on the market, and left the area as fast as she could get away.

"That would be good for Nora," Shelly said. "She wants to be as far from Paxton Park as she can get, and really, who could blame her? She told me she knew her son was a greedy, self-centered man, but she couldn't believe what he'd done and that it would take her a very long time to process Paul's terrible crimes. Nora said she needed the anonymity that living in a new place could give her."

"Understandable." Julie nodded. "I'd probably move away under the circumstances." The young woman straightened up and faced her friend with an expression of alarm. "I completely forgot to tell you. This morning, someone from the resort was up in the woods on the trails that lead to the Crooked

Forest. One of the trees has been damaged. Part of a limb has been sawed right off."

Justice hissed from her perch on the railing.

"What?" Shelly nearly gasped. "Can the tree be saved?"

The Crooked Forest was a grove of pines that grew up from the ground, turned at a ninety-degree angle and grew parallel to the ground, then turned again to vertical growth. Although the trees had been studied by botanists and other scientists, there was no definitive explanation for the unusual growth patterns.

"I'm not sure. Some experts were being called in to look at the damage and recommend how to care for the tree," Juliet said.

"Do they know who is responsible?"

"No," Juliet said. "No one was caught."

A cold shiver ran through Shelly's stomach like a warning of something bad to come. "The resort should post a guard up there for a while. The person who did it might come back." Anger flashed in her blue eyes. "Why would anyone do such a thing?"

Juliet shook her head in disgust. "Who knows?"

"I hope they catch the person." A chilly breeze came by and Shelly zipped up her sweater. "No one in town wants those trees to be damaged."

After eating an early dinner of chili and corn-bread, Shelly and Juliet headed off to town to walk around, take a look at the Halloween decorations on the common, and then go see a film at the movie theatre. It was a cool night in the mountain town and the young women wore light jackets to ward off the chill.

Walking under the streetlights, their shoes crunched on some of the fallen leaves as they joined people strolling by the stores. A yellow-orange, nearly full moon glimmered next to the stars sprinkled in the dark sky.

"I wonder if snow will show up sooner than usual this year." Juliet had her hands in her jacket pockets. "The skiers would love that."

Listening to her friend talk about skiing, Shelly became more aware of her limp. The cold temperatures seemed to make the aching worse. "Even though I enjoy it, I've never been a great skier. I haven't been on skis since the accident. I wonder how my leg injury will impact me."

Almost a year ago, Shelly had been in a devastating car accident in Boston that took the life of her twin sister, Lauren. After Shelly's injuries healed, she was left with aches and pains in her leg along with a most-likely permanent limp.

"Once you get back on your skis, it might not bother you at all." Juliet gave Shelly an encouraging smile. "It might just take a little practice to get back to form."

Reminded of the accident, a sense of gloom descended over Shelly and she deliberately forced her thoughts to happier things to push away her feelings of loss.

Passing the movie theatre on the way to the town common, Shelly began to feel anxious and as she gazed up at the movie posters in the windows, her body gave an involuntary shudder.

It was horror weekend at the theatre and they were going to see a scary movie later that evening. Frightening movies had never really bothered Shelly so she didn't understand why she felt flickers of unease as they walked past the theatre. She turned her head from side to side scanning the town for anything out of the ordinary, but nothing looked amiss.

The common was abuzz with tourists and locals gathered to admire the scarecrows set up around the green space. People were having their pictures taken with their favorites, parents held the hands of small children who seemed wary of some of the scarier scarecrows, and couples held hands as they marveled at the work that went into most of the creations.

Shelly and Juliet walked over the grass and pointed to the ones they liked the most. "How did they get it to stay up in the air like that?" Juliet asked.

"Smoke and mirrors," Shelly chuckled.

"I'm serious. How did they manage it?" Juliet strolled around the dollhouse that gave the impression it was floating in the air.

"Must be wires and transparent plastic piping," Shelly suggested as she peered underneath the floating dollhouse. "Maybe."

"A bunch of these scarecrow displays are so elaborate." Juliet eyed each one as they passed. "If we're going to enter next year, we'd better start planning now."

"Let's head back," Shelly said checking the time. "I bet the movie theatre will be crowded tonight."

Walking several blocks back to the theatre, the young women paused on the sidewalk before crossing the side street to continue over to the old-fashioned box office set at the entrance to the place. Someone called their names and they paused at the curb, looking over their shoulders to see a friend from the resort coming towards them.

A choking flood of fear raced through Shelly and

she wheeled around, stepped into the street, grabbed the arm of a middle-aged woman, and yanked her back onto the sidewalk.

The shaken woman was about to berate Shelly when a car careened around the corner, its right front wheel bumping up over the curb as it flew down the side street and crashed into the front of a brick building ... the noise of metal screeching as the vehicle crumpled and twisted on impact.

The collision's sickening shriek caused the remembered sounds of her own car crash to surface, and Shelly stood with her hands over her ears and her eyes pinched closed ... and a high-pitched scream letting loose from her throat.

2

_____

Shelly couldn't recall falling down onto the sidewalk and for a few seconds, she wasn't able to make out what Juliet was saying to her.

"Are you okay? Can you stand?" Juliet had her hand on her friend's arm and when Shelly nodded in response to the question, Juliet helped her stand up.

"What happened?" Shelly blinked in the direction of the crashed car.

"You saved my life." The auburn-haired middle-aged woman whom Shelly had grabbed and pulled to safety stood before her. "How did you know that car was coming? I never even saw it."

"I...." Shelly stared at the wrecked vehicle

watching two pedestrians hurry to help whoever was inside. "I must have heard the engine."

The woman gripped Shelly's hand and thanked her over and over. "If not for you, I surely would have been hit. I could have been killed." The woman's husband rushed over and listened as his wife reported what had happened while he'd been browsing in a men's clothing store.

Shelly and Juliet walked down the side street and approached the crashed car. The driver's side door was open and a man leaned inside to check on the occupant.

The man stepped back with an ashen face. They heard the alarm in his voice when he spoke. "She doesn't have a pulse. I can't find a pulse."

Edging closer, the two friends looked to see if they might be able to help.

"It's just the one person. It's only the driver inside," someone yelled from the passenger side. "No one else is in the car."

"Should we try to do chest compressions until the ambulance gets here?" a woman asked.

"I don't think we should lift her out," a man told the others. "We could make an injury worse by moving her."

The man who had checked the driver of the car stood straight. "There's.... She's...."

"What?" Juliet asked him. "What is it?"

The older man's eyes were wide. "It looks like the driver has a gunshot wound."

"Where is the wound?" An older woman who said she was a nurse hurried over and leaned into the vehicle for a few moments. When she stood up, her eyes were wide with concern. "I doubt the crash killed her. She has a bullet wound to the chest."

Shelly and Juliet exchanged looks of alarm.

Two police cars and an ambulance screamed up Main Street and took the corner down the side road. The onlookers moved back to let the officials take over. The nurse reported to the emergency personnel what appeared to be a gunshot wound.

The EMTs paused for a split second in surprise, and then they rushed forward to assist the car's occupant.

"She was shot?" Juliet turned to Shelly. "Who could have shot her? When? I didn't see anyone get out of the car after it crashed. I didn't see anyone near the car right after it stopped. Did you?"

"I was on my butt on the sidewalk," Shelly reminded her friend. "All I could see were legs and feet."

Juliet eyed Shelly. "How did you know to pull that woman out of the street?"

"I don't know. I barely remember doing it. Maybe I saw the car out of the corner of my eye. Maybe I heard the engine and sensed the car was too close." Shelly gave a helpless shrug.

Two people passed by and one said, "I heard the cop say that the driver is dead."

"From the bullet," Juliet said softly. "That must be why the car careened out of control."

Shelly narrowed her eyes and scanned the people standing around in the darkness on the sidewalks that lined the two streets. "How did someone shoot her? From where?"

"The police will figure it out," Juliet said as a third patrol car screeched to a stop. "There's Jay." Juliet's sister, Jayne Landers-Smyth, was a twenty-year veteran of the Paxton Park police department. Jay was fifteen years older than her younger sister, was two inches taller, and had a stocky build which made her look strong and formidable. Her chin-length hair was the same medium brown color as Juliet's.

When she got out of her police vehicle, Jay headed straight for the accident scene and did not notice her sister and Shelly standing on the sidewalk.

"I couldn't see much when we went over to offer help," Shelly said. "Did you see the woman's face? Did you recognize her?"

Juliet shook her head. "I didn't see her face." Looking back to the accident, she said, "I don't recognize the car, either."

"Do you want to go home?" Shelly asked. "I don't much feel like going to see the movie now."

"I'd rather head home, too. Let's go. This has given me a scare." Juliet rubbed her hands up and down the arms of her jacket trying to ward off the chill. "Is someone driving around with a gun in their car? Did someone pick this woman randomly or did the killer know who she was and seek her out?"

"Good questions. We'll have to wait for the answers."

"How did he do it?" Juliet asked as they walked along Main Street. "Was he in the car with her? Did he shoot her as she drove past him?"

"He'd have to be a pretty good shot if he hit her as she drove along." Shelly zipped up her jacket. "He couldn't have been standing on the sidewalk with a gun waiting for her to pass by. Someone would have seen him." She glanced at the buildings around them and looked up. Most buildings were two stories, but a few had three or four levels. "Was he up in a window on one of the higher floors?"

As they passed a coffee shop, Juliet gestured. "Want a coffee or some tea? I'm not ready to go home just yet."

The two went in and took seats by the windows. There were only a handful of customers inside, most had taken off to go to the accident scene to rubberneck.

Shelly wrapped her hands around the hot mug of tea and watched people walking past the window. "At first I thought the person driving the car might have had a heart attack and that was what caused the crash."

"I thought the woman just lost control of the car. It didn't cross my mind that she might have experienced a health problem," Juliet said. "I sure didn't think she'd been murdered."

Shelly blew out a long breath. "Murdered," she said thinking about the situation. "Could she have shot herself? Committed suicide?"

Juliet's blue eyes widened. "Suicide? Oh, I don't know. Wouldn't she have pulled over? Why would she do that in a moving vehicle?"

"Maybe she got bad news. She might carry a gun in her purse. Something may have upset her and she grabbed the gun out of her bag and then...." Shelly let her voice trail off. "It's possible, isn't it?"

Juliet huffed. "If that's what she did, she's lucky she didn't kill anyone in town." Sipping her tea, her eyes narrowed and she straightened up. "You know what? I think I do recognize that car. There's a woman who works at the resort, in the financial office. She's an accountant. She just got a new car." A look of apprehension raced over Juliet's face. "Oh, gosh. Is she the dead woman in that car?"

"What's her name?" Shelly asked.

"Emma. Emma Pinkley."

"I know who Emma is. I met her at a resort employee event. You think that was her car?" Shelly asked, her voice tinged with worry.

"What color was it?" Juliet wasn't sure she was correctly remembering the color of the car that crashed.

"Um, a dark color?" Shelly asked. "I can't be more specific than that. It's evening. It wasn't under a streetlamp."

"Let's go back and see." Juliet got up from her seat. "It just can't be Emma."

The two young women hurried the few blocks back to the accident scene. The road had been blocked off and an officer stood at the corner keeping people from wandering closer. Separate crowds of people stood on the sidewalks on opposite sides of the street watching what was going on.

Juliet stood on tiptoes trying to see over the people's heads. "What kind of a car is it?"

A man standing near the front told her the make and model of the crashed vehicle.

"What color is it?"

"Dark green," the man reported.

Juliet's hand flew to her mouth.

"Is that what Emma drives?" Shelly asked and when Juliet nodded, she tried to calm her friend. "Other people drive the same kind of car. It doesn't necessarily mean it's Emma's car."

"I bet it is though." Juliet's face had blanched. "I have a bad feeling about it."

Shelly asked the people standing around them, "Has the driver been identified?"

No one knew for sure.

A middle-aged man who was watching from the edge of the group moved closer to Shelly. "I was near the car right after it crashed. A few people rushed over to help. I offered to help them move the woman from the car, but they thought it was best not to jostle her. Someone took the wallet from her bag and found the license. The woman's name was Emma something. I didn't catch the last name."

Juliet groaned. "Oh, no."

Shelly slipped her arm through Juliet's and maneuvered her away from the crowded sidewalk.

"I can't believe it." Juliet shook her head. "I just talked to her yesterday. How could she be dead? Shot dead?"

"What do you know about her?" Shelly asked as they headed down the sidewalk towards home.

"Emma's in her early forties. Has two kids, a girl and a boy. One is seventeen, the other is fourteen. She lives at the edge of town."

"Is there a husband?" Shelly asked.

"Yes. Emma talked about him. His name is Charlie. He's an emergency room nurse at the hospital." Juliet stopped walking and wheeled to Shelly. "Oh, no. What if he's at work when they wheel Emma in? I don't know him well enough to call and tell him what happened."

Shelly touched her friend's arm. "Someone will figure it out. Someone will alert the husband so he knows what happened before they bring his wife in. Will they even bring her to the hospital? If she's already passed away?"

"I don't know." Juliet shook her head as she

started walking again. "What in the world could have caused someone to shoot Emma?"

"I'd bet Emma probably knew her attacker since she was in her car when she got shot," Shelly said. "At least, I bet she was in the car when it happened."

"So she must have slowed down or pulled over to talk to the person who did it."

"She couldn't have driven far with a gunshot to the chest," Shelly said. "Either she got shot while sitting in the car or maybe she was standing next to it when it happened."

"Why didn't she call for help?" Juliet asked. "Why did she drive away?"

"To get away from the person who shot her?" Shelly's fingers were freezing and she pushed her hands into her pockets.

"How far do you think Emma could have driven with an injury like that?"

Shelly shrugged. "I have no idea. It must depend on where the bullet hit her."

"Emma was such a nice person, always friendly and cheerful. Why would someone want to kill her?" Juliet wondered.

The same question was on Shelly's mind.

Why, indeed?

3

Early the next morning, Shelly, Juliet, and Jay sat around the small table eating eggs and toast in the screened room at the back of Juliet's cottage. Justice stared out through the screen at a few birds pecking at the grass under a shade tree in the backyard.

Jay had a late night working the car crash scene in the center of town. Juliet invited her older sister to come for breakfast to talk about the case.

"You already know that the woman, Emma Pinkley, was an accountant at the resort. She'd lived in this area her whole life." Jay took a swallow of her coffee. "We spoke with her husband last night ... of course, the guy was plenty shook up. He told us Emma left the house in the late afternoon to do

21

some shopping and errands and she was planning to have dinner at her mother's place over in Linville."

"Does anyone know what Emma did after leaving her mother's house?" Juliet asked.

Jay said, "We're going to speak with the mother in an hour. Last night, she said her daughter didn't stay for dinner as planned. The woman was so distraught over Emma's death that we weren't able to talk with her any further."

"So Emma cancelled dinner with her mother?" Shelly asked.

Jay nodded. "That's what the mother told us."

"But did Emma see her mother yesterday?" Shelly asked. "Did she stop by her mom's house even though she wasn't going to stay for dinner?"

"Unknown." Jay buttered her toast. "We'll find out the details when we talk to her later this morning."

"What about the gunshot wound?" Juliet made a face. "Was it self-inflicted?"

"Emma's husband, Charlie, claimed his wife did not own a gun," Jay said. "The medical examiner will let us know more about the wound ... but really? There was no gun found in the car and initial examination did not reveal anything on the woman's fingers or hands that might point to her turning a gun on herself. Right now, I'm inclined to believe Emma Pinkley was shot by someone other than herself."

Justice looked at the women gathered around the table and growled low in her throat.

"What about the husband?" Shelly questioned. "Was he at work around the time Emma was shot?"

"He was at work until late afternoon, but not in the evening."

"So he's a possible suspect then." Juliet sighed.

Jay turned her piercing blue eyes to Shelly. "Have you had any dreams lately?"

A shudder went through Shelly's body and her voice was soft when she answered. "None that seem important."

Ever since the fatal car accident, Shelly sometimes had dreams where her sister, Lauren, appeared and seemed to be trying to send her a message. Jay suggested that the dreams were probably Shelly's subconscious working to point out things she hadn't paid attention to during the day. Jay thought that Shelly might have a heightened sensitivity to or perception of people and situations and when her mind was quiet, her subconscious worked on problems or issues and highlighted in her dreams the things she'd overlooked or ignored in the day. Since moving to Paxton Park a few months ago, Shelly's dreams had pointed to several things that helped solve two recent murder cases.

"Have you had any dreams where Lauren was in them?" Jay asked gently, knowing that Shelly was bothered by the possibility she might have some special ability that most other people lacked.

"No." Shelly shook her head. Despite her negative reply, Lauren *had* been in several of her dreams recently, but there wasn't anything odd about them. Shelly and her sister had been enjoying a meal together at a restaurant sitting with some mutual friends. That was all that happened. Nothing seemed important or unusual or troubling about the dreams so Shelly didn't mention them.

"Okay." Jay seemed slightly disappointed.

Shelly noticed the look on Jay's face. "I didn't know Emma Pinkley well. I'd only met her a few times. I don't know anything about her. My sleeping mind wouldn't be able to highlight anything I've overlooked during the day because my brain doesn't have any information about the woman."

Juliet pointed out, "But you didn't know the murdered women in those recent cases and you were still able to help."

Shelly opened her mouth to protest, but then

closed it, not sure how to respond. After pausing for a few seconds, she said, "I heard about those women by talking to other people, by hearing from people who knew them or interacted with them. Somehow I picked up on things that helped."

Jay and Juliet exchanged a quick look, and then Jay shifted her gaze to Shelly. "I wonder ... if you talk to people who knew Emma, would you pick up on things that the rest of us will likely miss?"

"Probably not." Shelly forced a chuckle and attempted a joke. "I'm not a mind reader, you know."

"Would you like to sit in on the interview this morning with Emma Pinkley's mother?" Jay asked.

Feeling her stomach clench, Shelly said in a small voice, "I'm due at work in an hour."

"Could you go in a little later?" Jay looked hopeful.

Dreading the possibility of getting drawn into the case, Shelly quickly reached for the jar of jam. Her elbow bumped her juice glass and almost knocked it over, but Jay caught it before it spilled.

"Thanks," Shelly said.

"Anytime," Jay told her, and then added with a wink, "We help each other."

Letting out a sigh, Shelly said, "I'll call Henry at the diner and tell him I won't be in until later."

Emma Pinkley's mother lived in the next town over from Paxton Park in a neatly-tended ranch house. Nancy Billings, in her late sixties with short layered silver hair and light blue eyes, was about five feet four inches tall and carried a few extra pounds on her petite frame. The whites of her eyes were raw and red from crying and she gripped a mangled tissue in her hand. Her older daughter, Evelyn, sat on the sofa next to her, their shoulders touching.

Evelyn looked to be in her late forties. She had short blond hair cut in layers around her face and she had her mother's facial features and light blue eyes. The rims of Evelyn's eyes were bright pink and she flicked her gaze around the room as if she was looking for something that could anchor her and allow her to escape from her misery.

Shelly sat next to Jay on a sofa opposite the two women and wished she could run from the room. After introductions and condolences, Jay got down to the questioning.

"You and Emma had planned to have dinner together?" Jay used a gentle tone of voice.

Nancy's hand tightened over the tissue. "We were

going to, but Emma asked if I'd mind changing our plans to the next evening."

"Why did she change your plans?"

"She told me she was feeling rushed and still needed to go to the grocery store and do some errands. And, she was giving someone a ride somewhere."

"Do you know who she was giving a ride to?"

"She said a friend. I don't know who it was though." Nancy reached over to her older daughter and took her hand.

"Do you know where they were going?" Jay asked.

"I'm not sure. Emma said she had to drop the friend off somewhere."

"Was the friend a man or a woman?"

Nancy's shoulder moved up and down in a shrug. "I don't know."

"So you didn't see Emma last night?" Jay tried to clarify.

"I did, but only for a few minutes. She came by and dropped off some take-out food for me. She felt bad about canceling dinner and didn't want me to have to cook for myself." Nancy's face tightened and her lips clamped together to keep from dissolving into tears. "Emma was always so thoughtful."

"Do you know if Emma was worried about anything?" Jay questioned.

Nancy shook her head. "She didn't tell me anything like that. She seemed normal. Well, there was a man at Windsor Manufacturing that Emma didn't like. That was the place she worked part-time for a while. He seemed to want to go out with Emma. She said he sent her inappropriate messages, lewd, dirty stuff."

Shelly's eyes widened.

"Do you know his name?" Jay questioned.

"Steve. I don't know his last name."

"Did Emma have an argument with anyone recently?"

Evelyn gave her mother a sideways look. "Emma and her husband occasionally argued. Sometimes, there was trouble between them."

"Not lately," Nancy told them.

Jay made eye contact with Evelyn. "What sort of trouble?"

Evelyn said, "Charlie wasn't good with money. He liked to gamble. A couple of times he ran up some debt, a lot of it. Emma was furious. It caused their relationship some strain."

"Had Charlie been in trouble with debt recently?" Jay questioned.

"Not recently," Evelyn said. "Not that I know of anyway. The last time was about six months ago."

"Were Emma and Charlie considering splitting up?"

"It crossed Emma's mind that last time. She was fed up." Evelyn moved her fingers over her eyes.

"What state was the marriage in at the present time?" Jay asked.

Evelyn said, "Emma had lost respect for Charlie. He couldn't control his gambling. He wouldn't go for help."

"Was divorce in the picture?" Jay asked.

"I don't think so. They seemed to have settled into a routine. I think they stayed together for the kids' sakes. I don't think Emma would ever forgive Charlie for the mess he made of their finances, but she was pleasant to him when they were together."

"Was the gambling the only trouble they had?" Jay looked pointedly at Nancy and Evelyn.

"You mean did they have affairs? Did they cheat on each other?" Evelyn asked for clarification.

Jay nodded.

Nancy said, "Emma wouldn't engage in that behavior."

Jay leaned forward slightly. "So their disagreements were solely about money and gambling?"

"I think so," Evelyn said.

Nancy's lower lip trembled. "You don't think Charlie had anything to do with this, do you?"

Shelly's heart skipped a beat. Did Emma's mother have reason to believe Charlie might have the desire to kill Emma?

"We're only collecting information," Jay said with an easy manner. "We don't have any suspects as yet." After looking at Nancy for several seconds, Jay asked, "Do you and Charlie get along?"

Nancy bit her lip and brushed at her eyes before whispering, "I don't like him."

A flash of anxiety raced through Shelly's veins.

4

L ater that afternoon, Shelly and Juliet sat in uncomfortable wooden chairs in Jay's cubbyhole of a windowless office in front of the beat-up desk covered with folders, papers, and a laptop.

Jay said, "Preliminary information indicates Emma Pinkley was shot in the chest by someone. She did not commit suicide. She was shot while sitting in the driver's seat of her car. It's too early for a definitive answer, but an educated guess by the medical examiner tells us that Emma might have been able to drive the car for five, possibly ten minutes, before bleeding out or succumbing to her wound."

"That gives us a radius to work with to plot out where Emma could have been when she was shot," Juliet said.

"Possibly," Jay said. "It will narrow it down at least."

"Have any witnesses come forward? Did anyone see Emma driving into town?" Shelly asked.

"Nothing yet," Jay said while clicking on her mouse and staring at the laptop screen. "Based roughly on what the medical examiner told us about Emma's ability to drive while shot, I've got a map of the area here displaying a ring of possibility where the woman might have been attacked." Jay gestured for her sister and Shelly to come and have a look.

The young women hunched down behind Jay and trained their eyes on the map.

"She could have been in Linville where her mother lives," Shelly pointed out. "But her mother said Emma told her she was going to Paxton Park to do some errands."

"Emma might have been shot before getting back to town after seeing her mother," Juliet said.

"Do you know yet who Emma was supposed to be driving somewhere?" Shelly asked.

"Not yet." Jay's gaze was fixed on the map. "Emma wouldn't have been on the mountain with her car so we can eliminate this whole section that's in the woods or on the mountain. So that leaves Linville in this direction, Paxton Park in the middle, Rollingwood to the south, and West Rollingwood." Jay let out a sigh. "It's a lot of ground to cover."

"Do you have a list of Emma's friends?" Shelly asked. "And their addresses?"

"Working on it," Jay said. "We have an officer doing the leg work on that aspect of things. We'll also ask Emma's mother, sister, and husband about people Emma was close to and people she was friendly with, but maybe wouldn't classify as a friend."

"She could have been going to meet an associate from work and just used the word 'friend' when talking to her mother," Juliet said.

"What did her mother say?" Shelly asked. "Emma had to drop someone off somewhere?"

"That's what she said," Jay answered. "Although, Emma could have done that before going to see her mom."

"Any idea what errands Emma had to do?" Shelly asked.

"The mother didn't know." Jay looked through her folder for a piece of paper.

Shelly and Juliet returned to their seats.

Jay looked up. "Next on the agenda, I'll be talking to the husband and the two kids ... individually, of course." Eyeing Shelly, she asked, "Can you tag along?"

Shelly was careful not to let her true feelings show about attending the interviews with Emma's family members. "When will the interviews be?"

After Jay gave her the days and the times, Shelly, barely able to hide her reluctance, said, "I think I can go with you."

"I appreciate it." Jay gave the young woman a nod.

DECIDING to head over to the resort hoping to talk to some of the employees, Shelly and Juliet found a couple of adventure guides and two people from the accounting office sitting outside at a picnic table on the enormous deck that wrapped around several of the buildings.

"We can't believe Emma is dead," Leslie, one of the accountants, said when Shelly and Juliet sat down to join them. "And shot by someone? It's incomprehensible."

Robert, another accountant, rubbed at his eyes.

"Emma was such a good person. Who would kill her? Do you think it was random?"

"It could have been," Shelly said despite her feeling that Emma probably knew her killer.

"Does anyone know where it happened?" Brandon, one of the adventure guides, asked. "Do the police know where Emma was when the killer approached?"

"I don't think so," Juliet said. "I don't think the police know the location yet."

"Shot in the chest?" Andy, the other guide, asked, "How did Emma ever drive her car into town with an injury like that?"

"Where was she going?" Brandon questioned. "Why didn't she call the police or an ambulance?"

Juliet said, "Shelly thinks Emma might have been trying to get away from the killer. She was losing blood. She probably wasn't thinking straight. Her first impulse must have been to get away, and then she must have started to get weak and probably had to fight to remain conscious." Jay had told her sister and Shelly that initial reports pointed to the woman having been shot in the vehicle, but the information couldn't be shared with the others so Juliet stayed closed-mouthed about that detail.

Shelly faced the two accountants. "You worked closely with Emma?"

"We did," Leslie said.

"It's really hit us hard," Robert told them shaking his head.

"How was she to get along with?" Shelly asked.

"She was great," Leslie said. "Always helpful, accommodating, cheerful. She knew her stuff, was really smart."

Robert agreed. "Emma was the best."

Shelly sat up. "Was Emma working on anything difficult or maybe, controversial?"

Leslie narrowed her eyes. "What do you mean?"

"Was Emma investigating anything? Were there any discrepancies of some kind in the accounts?"

Leslie and Robert exchanged a look of concern.

"I don't know," Leslie said with a tremble in her voice. "I don't know what she was working on specifically."

"You think she was working on something that might have gotten her killed?" Robert's face took on a look of horror.

"It crossed my mind," Shelly admitted. "I wondered if she found something that maybe someone preferred to keep hidden."

Leslie's hand moved to her throat. "That can't be." She made eye contact with Robert. "Can it?"

Shelly could see Robert's chest rising and falling as his breathing rate increased. He didn't know how to answer his colleague's question. "What could she have been working on? Maybe we can find out?"

"We'll need to be careful," Leslie told him. "If there is trouble in the books, we don't want to put ourselves at risk."

"Don't do anything that would put you in danger," Shelly cautioned. "Don't push for answers."

Andy, the guide, asked, "How did Emma get along with her husband?"

"I don't know," Robert said. "I never talked to her about him. She did mention him from time to time in general conversation, like what they had planned to do for the weekend, things like that."

Leslie's expression had changed, and a look of anger, or maybe annoyance passed quickly over her face.

Shelly couldn't make out what emotion it was. "Did Emma talk to you about her husband?"

"Sometimes." Leslie's mouth seemed tight. "Charlie was kind of a pain in the butt."

"How do you mean?" Juliet asked. "Had you met him?"

"Only a few times." Leslie seemed to be wrestling with something. "Emma's husband wasn't an easy person. He liked to gamble and got himself into trouble with debts and money owed."

"Emma confided in you about it?" Juliet asked.

"We talked about a lot of things going on in our lives. Sometimes you just need someone to vent to, you know?"

"How did Emma handle the gambling?" Shelly asked.

"The first time, she tried to be understanding about it," Leslie said. "She felt like Charlie had gotten sucked into it. She wanted to help him." The woman sighed. "The second time, she wasn't so ready to forgive. Emma wanted Charlie to get counseling, but he wasn't really interested in going."

"Did this happen recently?" Juliet asked.

"Emma hadn't brought it up recently. The last time Charlie made a mess of things was about six months ago. It took Emma almost that long to get the debts paid off. She worked extra in the resort office. She even got a second job, part-time, to make money."

"Where did she work the second job?" Shelly asked.

Leslie said, "She worked in Rollingwood at a business called Windsor Manufacturing. She stopped working there about a month ago. It was only a short-term thing."

"Did she talk about the job there?" Juliet questioned.

"Yeah, she did. She said it was okay. The people weren't that friendly. Emma said working at Windsor made her grateful for the resort job."

"Did she ever complain about anyone in particular at Windsor?"

Leslie's forehead furrowed in thought. "Emma said one of the women in the office wasn't very friendly. Once, she tried to blame Emma for something that Emma had nothing to do with. She said she had to keep an eye on that person."

"Did Emma mention being afraid of anyone there? Did she get into an argument with anyone?" Was anyone threatening in any way?"

"No, nothing like that came up. Emma was looking forward to not having to work there. It was a really long day for her. I think she resented Charlie for not doing enough to help eliminate the debt, especially since it was all his fault."

Juliet leaned forward and kept her voice low. "Do

you think Charlie might have had something to do with Emma's death?"

Leslie bit her lip and swallowed. "There are some people I would say *absolutely not, he couldn't have killed her, no way*, but with Charlie? Really? I don't know. I can't be sure. I just don't trust that guy."

5

R esting in bed with a book propped on her lap and with Justice curled up next to her, Shelly pushed the death of Emma Pinkley from her mind and thought about meeting Jack the next morning for a bike ride on the mountain trails. She and her boyfriend both had part of the morning off from work and Shelly looked forward to a brisk ride through the forest to clear her head and renew some of her energy.

Not long ago, she'd assisted Jay with a case involving the disappearance and murder of a young woman from town and the crime had taken a toll on her. Still healing physically and emotionally from the car accident that took her sister's life, Shelly realized the need to carefully balance her time between her part-time bakery job, helping Jay on cases, and having downtime to enjoy herself in order to maintain her health and well-being.

It had been a long day and it was almost 11:30pm, but Shelly wanted to stay awake to finish the chapter of the thriller she was reading. The need for sleep was winning the battle though, as her heavy eyelids kept drifting shut until finally her eyes closed, her chin hit her chest, and the book slipped from her hands.

Justice moved onto the young woman's stomach where she curled into a ball and joined Shelly in sleep.

A dream began....

Shelly, her sister, Lauren, and several other women sat at a round table in a crowded pub, eating dinner, chatting, and laughing together. Lauren's blue eyes sparkled when she chuckled at a joke. She passed a piece of garlic bread to Shelly, and Shelly reciprocated by lifting a small section of lasagna from her own plate to her sister's. The waiter carried over a tray and set drinks in front of the friends.

A glass of red wine had been placed next to Shelly's water glass and she glanced at it, but did not drink. Lauren picked up the wine glass, waved the waiter over, and handed it to him to take away.

Suddenly, paper money began to float down from the ceiling ... hundreds, thousands of bills drifted around the restaurant patrons, but no one except Shelly paid any attention to the strange sight. The currency began to move together like a flock of birds gathering in the sky and then they started to swirl creating a small cyclone of green dollar bills that shot up to the rafters and disappeared.

A framed painting fell off the restaurant's wall and crashed to the floor, its glass shattering into tiny shards.

Shelly woke with such a sudden start that Justice jumped up and hissed.

Disoriented and with her heart pounding, Shelly's eyes darted around the bedroom until she realized where she was, leaned back on her pillow, and reached out to pat her sweet cat. "I had a dream," she told the Calico. "It was a strange one."

Justice eyed the young woman, then snuggled close, and began to purr. The comforting sound slowly calmed Shelly until she turned off the side table lamp, pulled her blanket up to her chin, and closed her eyes.

SHELLY AND JACK flew over the downhill trail on their bikes with the trees flashing past in a blur and the cool morning air rushing against their faces turning their cheeks bright red. When they reached the bottom, they stopped and sipped from their water bottles.

"That was great." Shelly pushed the dribbles of sweat from her forehead. "The downhill was sure a lot faster than the uphill climb," she chuckled.

"A lot faster and a lot easier." Jack smiled, pulled off his helmet, and ran his hand through his damp chestnut-colored hair. "And a great way to start the day." Leaning over his handle bars, Jack gave Shelly a kiss.

After parking their bikes in the metal stand, they strolled hand-in-hand to the resort café where they bought a muffin to share and two cups of hot tea and then carried them outside to eat on the deck in the sunshine.

Jack stretched his legs out in front of him and took a sip of the tea as he gazed up at the mountains towering above them. "Snow will fall on the mountain in a month or so and the skiers and snowboarders will descend. Winter is a terrific time in Paxton Park with all the outdoor activities."

"I want to try to ski again," Shelly rubbed her

sore leg absent-mindedly. Some slight pain always kicked in after doing anything athletic.

Jack smiled and reached over to take Shelly's hand. "Start slow, a little at a time. Don't rush it and go right to the summit on the first day. Take your time. Thirty minutes the first day on an easy trail so you can get back into it. You'll be at the top in no time."

Shelly smiled at the rugged man. "I think that's the way to do it."

"And I'll be right there beside you," Jack beamed. "We'll do it together."

While sharing the blueberry muffin, the two chatted about work and the upcoming weekend activities.

"What a thing to happen to Emma Pinkley," Jack said shaking his head. "Did you know her?"

"I'd only met her a few times." Shelly held the warm teacup with both hands.

"Same for me. The few times we talked at a resort event she was always really pleasant. She seemed like a nice woman. Who could have been out to kill her?"

"Did you know Emma's husband?" Shelly asked.

"I met Charlie when he kayaked and biked a few times with a group of guys I know. That was a couple of years ago. He liked to talk. My first impression was he seemed kind of full of himself." Jack shrugged. "But I didn't know him well at all."

"Someone I talked to told me Charlie had a gambling problem that put some strain on the marriage," Shelly said.

"I heard that through the grapevine. I didn't know if it was true or not."

"It seems to be true. I've heard it from several sources."

Jack looked over at Shelly. "Are you helping Jay again?" Shelly had talked with Jack at length about how Jay thought she had the special intuitive skill of being able to sense things about situations and people. Jack had told Shelly that there were some people in the military who seemed to have similar skills and that they were taken seriously and listened to.

"She asked if I would sit in on a few interviews with people who knew Emma," Shelly said.

"Try not to get swallowed up by this one," Jack said softly and held her hand tightly. "You need to be careful to take care of yourself and not just throw everything you've got into the case."

Shelly gave a half-smile. "It's hard not to do that when someone has been murdered."

"I understand, but you need to be sure you get enough sleep and eat well. Take breaks. Don't let the thing consume you. It hasn't even been a year since the accident," Jack pointed out. "If you're going to fully heal, you can't deplete your energy." The man gave his girlfriend a cheeky smile. "How about I come over Thursday night and cook dinner for you?"

"I won't say no to that," Shelly told him.

Someone called to them. "Hey, you, two. Working hard, I see." Dave Millbury, an amiable, middle-aged man who had been employed at the resort as an adventure guide for over twenty years ambled over to Shelly and Jack and took a seat in a white Adirondack chair across from them.

The three of them spent a few minutes talking about work and then Dave asked with a shake of his head, "Can you believe what happened to Emma? It's all everyone is talking about."

"Do people have any suspects in mind?" Shelly asked.

"Everybody has an opinion. Who knows, but can you imagine driving your car after being shot in the chest?" Dave let out a low whistle of amazement. "It's a heck of a thing. Emma must have been trying to get to the police station for help. Do you think so?"

"It might have been better to have slipped out of

the car once she reached the edge of town, where people were walking around. Someone could have called an ambulance," Jack said. "She was losing blood though so she most likely wasn't thinking anything through. She just wanted to get away from whoever shot her."

"Makes sense." Dave nodded solemnly. "What a thing. Emma was a great gal."

"You knew her pretty well?" Shelly asked.

"I've been working here for years. Emma, too. We'd run into each other. Shoot the breeze. She was such a nice person." Dave blew out a breath. "She worked hard, took care of her family. She sure didn't deserve this."

"Do you know her husband?" Shelly questioned.

Dave looked over at the young woman. "I don't have the same nice things to say about him."

"Why not?" Jack asked.

"Charlie is a child. Once in a while when we talked, Emma let some things out in frustration about the guy. He couldn't keep a dollar in his pocket. He gambled, spent everything he had. He drank, he bought old cars he planned to fix up, but never did anything with them. He always had some scheme. All of the schemes involved losing money." Dave's face took on an expression of disgust. "Emma was the rock in that house. She worked hard to pay off Charlie's debts. I think she'd had it with him."

"Did she talk about this stuff recently?" Shelly asked.

"I hadn't run into her in a while," Dave said. "I don't know where things stood as far as Charlie went, but I'd guess they were the way they usually were."

"Did Emma ever mention divorce?" Shelly questioned.

"Never. I don't know how she put up with Charlie. I'd have given him the boot a long time ago. She must have stayed with him for the sake of the kids. But really? So many money problems, drinking, chasing tail. She should have dumped him."

Shelly stared at Dave. "You mean Charlie had an affair?"

"Probably more than one. He couldn't keep away from the ladies."

"Emma told you this?" Shelly couldn't believe Emma would open up about all Charlie's woes to a work associate.

"No, no. Emma told me about the gambling and Charlie's stupid business schemes. She never said a word about Charlie's wandering eye. I've seen the guy in action in some pubs and I've heard some talk about him not being able to keep his hands to himself."

"Do you think Emma knew about her husband's behavior?" Shelly's eyes narrowed.

Dave raised an eyebrow. "She'd have to be blind not to know."

6

Seventeen-year-old Aubrey Pinkley had long, straight, light brown hair, big blue eyes, and an athletic build. Shelly could see a bit of Emma in the teen's face.

Jay thought it best to meet with Aubrey at the family home instead of at the police station so she would feel more comfortable.

"Would you like to sit out on the front porch to talk?" Aubrey asked with a smile and a gesture, and the three of them sat down at the small wooden table. Shelly noted the pleasant and polite manner of the teenager who had lost her mother just a few days ago and wondered if she was bottling up her emotions and burying them inside.

Jay and Shelly offered condolences and Jay

began the interview. "When did you last speak with your mother?"

Aubrey seemed to collect herself by taking in a breath and straightening her posture. "Just before she went out for the evening, on the day she --." Aubrey cleared her throat. "On the day she died."

"How was your mother's mood that day?" Jay asked.

"She seemed normal." Aubrey made steady eye contact with Jay. "She was her usual self. She always had a lot to do."

"And where was the rest of the family during the evening?" Jay questioned.

"I was here at home doing homework. My brother, Mason, was at a friend's house for a while and then he came home. Dad was out. He went shopping for new boots."

"What time was it when your brother and father arrived home?"

Aubrey screwed up her face. "Let's see. Mason came home about 8pm and Dad came in around 10:30pm, I'd say."

"Where did your father go to shop?"

"He went to the Country Mall in Stockville." Aubrey gave a nod.

"I believe the mall closes at 9pm. Did your father mention if he stopped somewhere on the way back?"

"No, he didn't."

"What kind of mood was he in when he got home?"

"The usual. I was upstairs in my room doing homework. He called up the stairs to me and told me he was home." Aubrey gave a shrug. "I told him I was working on an essay."

"And how about Mason?" Jay asked. "How was his mood when he got home?"

"Mason was a little cranky. He had a lot of work to do for school, but he didn't feel like doing it."

"Did you talk to him when he got back?"

"He stopped at my bedroom door. He complained about school. That was it. Then he went to his room. He put some music on. I could hear it through the wall."

"What about the day?" Jay asked. "Did anything out the ordinary happen before you got home from school?"

"Nothing. It was a regular day."

Your mother and father went to work?"

Aubrey nodded. "Yeah. Mason and I went to school and came home on the bus at the usual time.

Mason went to a friend's house for a while and I stayed home."

"Did your mother arrive home at her usual time?"

"She did. Well, she stopped at the mini-mart for a few things. She was going to our grandma's house for dinner so she got some burgers and rolls for us. Mom and Grandma and my aunt usually got together for dinner once a week, usually Friday nights. She was going to do some shopping and errands after she had dinner with Gram."

"Who made your dinner?" Jay asked.

"I was going to, but Dad came home a little early and he cooked the burgers. We ate together and then Dad left to go out. Mason ate at his friend's house."

"Did your mother cancel her plans with your grandmother before she left the house?"

Aubrey blinked. "I didn't know she cancelled her plans. Where did she go?"

"We wondered if you overheard anything about that," Jay told the teenager.

"I didn't, no." Aubrey's eyes were huge. "Mom didn't go to Grandma's for dinner?"

"She didn't. She rescheduled dinner for the next evening."

"Why didn't she go?" Aubrey tilted her head, concern etched into her forehead.

"We aren't sure. She told your grandmother she had things to do. She had to give someone a ride some place."

Aubrey considered the comment.

"Do you know which friend it might be that she needed to drive somewhere?" Jay asked.

"She didn't tell me. I don't know who she was driving. Did she tell my grandma who it was?"

"Your grandmother didn't know who she was meeting." Jay gave the girl an easy smile. "Who were some of your mom's friends?"

"Peggy and Monica ... and sometimes she went out with a friend named Leena, but I've never met her. Mom met Leena at the gym."

"Your mother worked out?" Jay asked.

Aubrey nodded. "Mom went to the gym before work twice a week. She used the treadmill. Sometimes she took a yoga class."

"That's where she met Leena?"

"Yeah. About a two months ago."

Jay asked for the last names of the three women who were friends of Emma. Aubrey told her Peggy and Monica's last names, but she did not know Leena's.

"You've met Peggy and Monica?"

"Oh, yes."

"Had your mother seemed worried about anything lately?"

"No." Aubrey shook her head. "She seemed normal."

"Did she complain about anyone? Did she have an argument with anyone?" Jay asked.

"She didn't tell me anything like that," Aubrey said.

"How did your father and mother get along?"

"Good. They got along good."

"Did you ever hear or see them argue?" Jay asked.

"No, I didn't."

"Did they seem annoyed with one another lately?"

Aubrey gave a shrug. "Maybe, once in a while."

"Did they ever have words with each other over anything? Money? The people they hung out with? Work schedules? Chores around the house?" Jay asked.

"I don't think so."

"Did your mother ever confide in you something about your father?"

A look of confusion washed over Aubrey's face. "Like what sort of thing? What do you mean?"

"Nothing in particular." Jay changed the subject. "How did you and your mother get along?"

Aubrey's face lit up. "We got along great. I loved her. She was the best."

"Did you get into arguments sometimes? Over clothes, boys, schoolwork?"

"We didn't. I know a lot of teenagers don't get along with their parents, but we did. We talked, did things together." Aubrey's face fell and Jay and Shelly could see some tears gather. The young woman bit her lower lip and then took in a few deep breaths. "My mom was really good to me," she said in a tiny voice and twisted her index finger in some strands of her long hair.

Shelly's heart ached for Aubrey's loss.

Jay moved the topic of conversation to something else. "Was your mother happy in her job?"

Aubrey's eyebrows raised slightly. "She liked working at the resort. She'd been there for a long time."

"Did she get along with her co-workers?" Jay asked.

"Yeah, she did. She told me a few times that she was really lucky to have that job. It was close to home, it paid well, the people were nice to work with. She enjoyed the work."

"I understand she had a second job?" Jay asked.

"For a little while, she did. She worked part-time, in the evenings, at Windsor Manufacturing over in Rollingwood."

"Why did she need to work two jobs?" Jay asked.

"Mom wanted the extra money to pay off some bills."

"Was she able to pay off the bills like she wanted to?" Jay and Shelly knew the bills probably had to do with Charlie's gambling.

"I think so," Aubrey said. "The job was temporary."

"Had your mother finished up working there?"

"The job ended a couple of weeks ago," Aubrey said. "Mom was glad it was over. She went out with some friends to celebrate."

"Did she go out with Peggy and Monica?" Jay asked.

"I'm pretty sure they went ... and some other people, too."

"Do you know who they were?" Jay asked.

"I don't know if she ever said. I'm not sure. People from work maybe."

"Did your father go to the celebration?"

"The get-together was only for women. Mom said so."

"Did your father work two jobs to help with the bills? Did he pick up extra shifts at the hospital?" Jay asked.

Aubrey shook her head. "No. He worked his regular schedule."

"I wonder why he didn't work extra to help with the bills?" Jay pressed.

"I don't know. Maybe the hospital didn't have any extra time to give him?"

"That could be," Jay nodded.

"When did your mother go out to celebrate?" Shelly asked the question.

Aubrey thought for a moment. "It was about two weeks ago. It was a Tuesday night. I remember because my friend invited me over to watch one of my favorite shows."

"Did you get home before your mom?" Shelly questioned.

"I did."

"Can you remember when your mom got home? Did she mention who was there at the restaurant?"

"She didn't."

"Did she tell you about the celebration?"

"No, she didn't say anything. Mom was really sick

when she got home. She came down with the flu or something. She could barely crawl to her room."

"That's terrible," Shelly said. "Did the flu last long?"

"Mom was in bed for two days. She could barely speak she was so sick. The shades had to stay down in her room … she had a bad headache. She slept for the two whole days."

"Was it a migraine?" Jay asked.

"Mom didn't get migraines. It was a headache from the flu, I guess."

"Was she okay after that?"

"She got up and was able to walk around and have something to eat. After taking another day to rest, she went back to work."

"Did any of the rest of you catch it?" Shelly asked.

"No, none of us. We were lucky. Mom was the only one who got sick."

Shelly couldn't put her finger on it, but something about the story didn't seem right.

7

Shelly worked at the long stainless steel table on one wall of the diner's kitchen. The kitchen served both the diner on one side and the resort bakery on the other. Shelly had been hired to bake breads and sweets for both places and she enjoyed the early morning banter with Henry, the diner's cook.

In their early seventies, Henry and his wife, Melody, had been leasing the diner from resort management for years and had been living in Paxton Park for even longer.

"What are you making this morning?" Henry asked his kitchen buddy while he manned the grill cooking eggs, bacon, pancakes, and home fries for the early customers.

"Sweet rolls, a chocolate cake, and some pies." Shelly added eggs to a mixture in the large bowl.

Before the diner's doors opened for the day, Henry, Melody, and Shelly had discussed the death of Emma Pinkley.

"That poor woman," Melody clucked. "She must have run into a nut."

"Why do you think it was random?" Shelly asked. "Couldn't the killer be someone she knew?"

"Emma was a good person, friendly, easy-going, nice to everyone. Who would want to kill her? She's the last person someone would hate or have a grudge against." Melody shook her head as she filled the salt and pepper shakers. "It had to be someone who didn't know her."

Shelly considered the possibility that an unknown assailant approached Emma and shot the woman ... that sort of thing happened everywhere, big cities, small towns. An unlucky person crossed paths with a killer looking for a victim. Is that what happened to the well-liked, middle-aged accountant? Did someone stand by their car on the side of the road and pretend they needed help? Did Emma stop to assist? Is that the reason she was shot while sitting in her own car? For no other reason than having had the misfortune of running into someone with murder on their mind? Shelly let out a sigh.

"How did you know Emma?"

"She and I were in a book group together," Melody said. "Last year, we were in the same water-color painting class."

Turning to face Melody with an expression of surprise, Shelly said, "I didn't know you painted."

Melody waved her hand around. "I'm not good at it, but I find it relaxing."

"She *is* good at it," Henry said from the grill. "She's too modest."

Melody smiled and shook her head. "I have a fan. One. But Henry doesn't count because he thinks I can do no wrong."

"Well, she *can* do wrong," Henry said keeping his eyes on the eggs he was frying. "But I pretend I don't notice. That keeps both of us happy."

Shelly chuckled at the older couple's banter.

"Do you know Emma's husband?" Shelly asked.

Melody's facial expression changed as she stacked coffee mugs on a tray. "I've met him. I've also heard about him."

"What have you heard?" Shelly looked sideways at Melody.

"Charlie has issues. He loves to gamble. He loves

to go out and have a few drinks. I'm not sure the words *a few* accurately describe his drinking. I've also heard he had an affair."

"Emma knew all these things?" Shelly asked.

"She told me about their financial mess," Melody said. "She told me about Charlie's gambling. It sort of slipped out one day when we were setting up for the book club at the library. Emma started to cry. She was embarrassed about becoming emotional, but she wanted me to understand why she'd broken down in tears so she gave me the two-minute condensed version of Charlie's gambling problem and what it had done to their finances."

Shelly leaned her hip against the work table. "Did she ever speak about it again?"

"No, and I didn't want to bring it up. I thought if she wanted to talk, she would have initiated a conversation. I got the feeling she regretted revealing the problems so I let it alone."

"How did you hear that Charlie had an affair?" Shelly asked. "Emma didn't mention that to you, did she?"

"Gosh, no. I heard it through the grapevine. I don't know if Emma was aware of Charlie's antics or not."

"I wonder if she knew, but didn't want to admit it to anyone," Shelly said.

"That's very possible."

"Do you know who he was involved with?" Shelly asked.

"I didn't hear names." Melody gave Shelly a look and rolled her eyes. "I heard he might have been involved with more than one woman."

Shelly groaned and went back to making a pie crust. "Do you know any of Emma's friends?"

"I know Monica. I think they've been friends for a very long time. She comes in here for coffee or breakfast most mornings. She hasn't been in since Emma died though."

Shelly was surprised to hear that Monica was a diner regular. Staying in the back workroom to bake, she never had the chance to get a good look at the diner's clientele and rarely interacted with any of them. "What's Monica like?"

"Monica's a park ranger. She lives in Paxton Park, but she works on the far north side of the mountain. I like her. She's always nice to talk with."

"I'd like to talk to her about Emma," Shelly said. "Would you point her out to me whenever she comes in again?"

Melody didn't ask Shelly why she wanted to talk to Monica. She just nodded and said, "I sure will."

As it turned out, Monica came to the diner for breakfast that morning and chose to sit in a booth up against the far wall. She sat on the bench with her back to the rest of the room.

Melody reported that the woman usually preferred one of the tables in the middle of the diner in order to chat with the other customers. "She probably doesn't want to hear the chatter and gossip about Emma."

Shelly asked, "Should I wait for another day to talk to her?"

"I'll introduce you. Play it by ear. If Monica seems uncomfortable, then cut it short."

After the introduction, Shelly sat down opposite the park ranger. "I hope you don't mind if I talk to you about Emma. I was in town that night. I was right there when her car crashed. We wanted to help, but...."

Monica took a deep breath and bit her lower lip.

Shelly went on. "I ... well, it was terribly upsetting to witness the crash. I only met Emma a few times. I've heard everyone say she was a really nice person. How did you know her?"

Monica trained her gaze on her plate. "Emma grew up in Paxton Park. My family moved here when I was thirteen. Emma was the first friend I made. I was shy back then. Emma was friendly to me on the first day of school. We hit it off right away."

"You and Emma were friends for a long time." Shelly gave the woman a gentle smile.

"We were." Monica gripped her water glass. "I can't believe what's happened. You didn't notice anyone suspicious that night, did you?"

Shelly shook her head. "Really? The whole thing happened so fast, I wouldn't have noticed anyone who seemed suspicious. I felt dazed from seeing the accident. Everyone's focus that night was on wanting to help Emma."

Monica let out a long breath of disappointment. "From what I've heard, no one seems to have seen a thing."

"The police think Emma was shot within a three to five-mile radius of where the car crashed. If that's the case, she was probably shot in a less-crowded location. Maybe somewhere more isolated."

"And then she drove into town?" Monica asked. "I heard people talking about that, but I didn't think it was possible for someone to drive for miles after being so badly injured."

"The medical examiner believes it could be done," Shelly said. "It wouldn't take very long to drive a few miles."

"You think Emma was going for help?"

"Maybe, or she was just trying to get away from her attacker." Shelly paused for a few moments. "Did Emma seem distracted by anything lately? Worried, anxious? Feeling down?"

"Not really," Monica said. "She'd been working two jobs. She was pretty worn out by the schedule. She was quieter than usual when we got together last. I chalked that up to her fatigue."

"When did you see her last?" Shelly inquired.

"About two weeks ago. I had to go to Boston for some training the week before Emma died so I didn't see her at all that week. We texted almost every day though."

"Did she seem like herself in the texts?"

"Yeah, she did. The texts were brief. *How was I doing? Was I enjoying the training?* She told me what was going with her. Things like that. The usual banter between friends."

"Why was she working two jobs?" Shelly asked.

She knew the answer, but wanted to hear what Monica had to say on the matter.

Monica's expression darkened. "Emma was trying to pay off some bills that had accumulated. Their financial situation was kind of in a mess."

"Did they take on a big loan? Was that the cause?"

Monica made eye contact with Shelly. "Charlie has a gambling problem. He ran up the debts."

"I see," Shelly said. "Was the marriage in danger because of that?"

Monica rested her chin on her palm. "Some days I thought *this is the end of the marriage*, then other days, it seemed things would work out okay. I don't know what would have happened to the marriage if Emma hadn't passed away. I'm not sure how things would have ended up."

"Was that the first time Charlie got into debt?"

Monica scowled. "No. This was the second time, and the debt was much worse. Emma was a good saver. She was always careful with money. This time, the savings got wiped out and it didn't cover the whole mess. That's why Emma took on the second job. She really did not like working there. She was relieved when it was done. She told me the people there were very unfriendly. One woman was jealous of her, tried to blame things on Emma. The supervisor was difficult. She couldn't wait to get out of there."

"Do you know the name of the woman who was giving Emma a hard time?" Shelly questioned.

Monica's brow creased in thought. "It was Danni something or other."

"Did Charlie do more shifts at the hospital to help pay off the debts?"

Monica made a huffing sound. "Are you kidding? Charlie is a selfish brat. He couldn't help with anything. He caused the problems and Emma cleaned them up. I can't stand him. I can't stand his behavior."

"Does he have other issues besides gambling?"

Monica raised an eyebrow. "Charlie cheated on Emma."

Shelly's eyes widened. "Did she know what was going on?"

"She did. She would have left him, but she hesitated because of the kids."

"Was it some one-time thing?"

Monica shook her head. "It was an affair. It went on for almost a year. It happened about a year ago. Emma found out about it and gave Charlie an ultimatum, quit seeing the woman or get out. He stopped seeing her ... so he said."

"Did Emma know who Charlie was seeing?"

"She knew. If he was my husband, I'd never trust Charlie again."

"Do you think he was still cheating on Emma? Do you think he was still seeing other women?"

Monica made eye contact with Shelly and said pointedly, "Like I said, I'd never trust Charlie again. With anything."

8

―――――――

Shelly worked in the kitchen of the Glad Hill Farm and Orchard making pies for the General Store. She'd been hired to work a few hours a week through the Christmas season so the farm wouldn't run short of pies to sell during the busiest months of September through December.

On the outskirts of town, the farm and orchard covered just over five hundred acres and depending on the season there were hayrides or sleigh rides for customers to enjoy. There was also a corn maze, a petting zoo, and a food barn selling products from the farm, and serving lunch, snacks, and ice cream.

The first time Shelly saw the food barn and general store inside the barn, she was amazed at the interior with the gleaming wooden walls and soaring ceilings with crystal chandeliers hanging from the rafters. There were huge windows on one side of the walls and the barn doors could slide back and open to a beautiful view of the landscape and the mountains beyond.

About a month ago, the owner of the farm and orchard, Dwayne Thomas, in his seventies, thin and wiry with a headful of white hair was deliberately being over-medicated by his nephew, Paul. Paul's plan was to make Dwayne appear feeble and forgetful and unable to run the business so that he could take the business over himself.

Paul attempted to force Dwayne to overdose, but Shelly was in the house with the older man and prevented the situation. Paul attacked Shelly and she came close to being killed. Dwayne spent two weeks in the hospital and came out almost as good as new.

Shelly put some pies into the commercial ovens and checked her watch for the time they'd need to come out, then she went outside to look for Dwayne.

Every sunny day in the late afternoon, Dwayne enjoyed sitting on the bench next to the lake where he could look out over the water, the green meadows, and off to the mountain range in the distance.

"Afternoon," Shelly greeted the man. "How are you doing?"

"Well, if it isn't my hero," Dwayne told the young woman. "I'm doing better every day."

Shelly shook her head with a smile, sat down next to Dwayne, and gave him a hug. "I've told you a bunch of times. I'm not a hero. We helped each other."

"I didn't help anyone with anything. You saved my life."

"And you telling me your suspicions about Paul's behavior helped the police determine that Paul had murdered Abby Jackson," Shelly said. Dwayne's nephew had kidnapped and killed a young woman from town who he'd fallen for, but who did not return the attraction.

Ever since she'd visited the man in the hospital, Shelly and Dwayne had been good-naturedly arguing over which one of them had done the most for the case.

"There's no point in debating this," Dwayne said. "You are the hero. I don't want to hear another word."

"Fine." Shelly chuckled. "It's nice to have you back to normal and sharp as a tack."

"What's the news on Emma Pinkley?" Dwayne asked. "Hard to believe another crime has been committed in town so soon after Abby's murder.

What's wrong with the world?"

"The police don't have any suspects yet. They're interviewing people who knew Emma. Did you know her?"

"I knew her well enough to say hello to and chat with for a little while. She grew up here in town. She was a very nice person." Under his doctor's suggestion, Dwayne was using a cane in the afternoons when he became tired. It was only until he'd regained all of his strength, the man told everyone. Dwayne lifted the cane and jabbed the bottom of it into the dirt. "Who would want to hurt poor Emma?"

"Do you know Emma's husband?"

"Charlie," Dwayne said with disgust. "A piece of work that one is. Charlie's problem is he has never grown up. He's immature. What Emma saw in that guy is beyond me. I don't know how he'll manage without Emma's steady presence."

"Some people think Emma stayed with Charlie because of the kids."

Dwayne grunted.

"I heard Charlie had cheated," Shelly said.

"Not a bit surprised. I've seen him in action in some pubs over the years. Charlie thinks all women are in love him. Such arrogance, and such disregard for his wife and family. You've heard about his gambling problem?"

Shelly nodded and then let her eyes wander over the beauty of the towering pines, the impossible blue of the sky, and the crystal clear lake trying to lessen some of the tension she felt when discussing the case. "Have you heard any talk about who could be the killer?"

"I've heard plenty of talk ... none of it has any basis in fact." Dwayne rolled the top of his cane in his hands. "But, I will share a fact with you."

Shelly shifted on the bench to better face Dwayne.

"When I was in the hospital, I saw Charlie there several times. Once, it was late at night. I didn't really see him, I heard him talking in the hallway outside my room. I couldn't sleep and was just resting in my bed."

"What did you hear?" Shelly asked.

"Charlie was on his break from the emergency room. He was talking to another nurse. The other nurse said something like *why don't you just divorce her then*? Charlie responded with something to the effect that he'd love to, but then he'd have to pay alimony and that his salary would go down to nothing. They moved away down the hall and I couldn't hear anything more."

"How can you be sure it was Charlie?" Shelly asked.

"I know his voice. Anyway, the other nurse said his name. It was Charlie, all right. Sounded like he would have loved to divorce Emma, but having less money was holding him back."

A flash of anxiety washed over Shelly. *Was Charlie cheating again? Did Charlie kill Emma to get rid of her? So he wouldn't have to pay alimony and would be free to do whatever he wanted ?* Shelly's heart beat sped up. *Did Emma have life insurance?*

"What do you think of that conversation I heard in the hospital?" Dwayne asked. "Probably the same thing I've been thinking?"

"That Charlie had something to do with Emma's death?" Shelly asked.

"The thought has crossed my mind." Dwayne tapped his cane against the ground.

"It's an interesting thought." Shelly's stomach seemed to fill with ice. "It wasn't that long ago when you heard Charlie say that stuff."

"No, it wasn't, but it was long ago enough that Charlie would have had plenty of time to plan and execute the crime," Dwayne said.

Shelly swallowed hard. "You've interacted with Charlie. You know him a little. Do you really think he is capable of murdering someone ... murdering his wife?"

Thinking of his nephew, Paul, and how he killed Abby Jackson and attempted to kill Shelly, Dwayne looked the young woman in the eye. "Sometimes, people's actions can surprise you, can't they?"

SHELLY BIKED from the farm back to her rented cottage on the quiet side street off of the main road in town. Juliet's car wasn't in her driveway which meant she was most likely still working at the resort. Shelly wanted to talk over what she'd learned from Dwayne and hoped her friend would get back soon.

Inside the bungalow, Justice met the young woman at the door and wound around Shelly's legs, purring.

"What a nice greeting." Shelly bent to scratch behind Justice's ears. "It's been a long day, kitty."

After getting a snack and a cup of tea, Shelly looked out the side window to Juliet's driveway, but her friend had not yet returned home.

With a sigh, Shelly plopped onto the sofa on her

back and rested her head against the soft decorative pillow. The Calico cat jumped up onto her owner's stomach and touched her tiny pink nose to Shelly's causing the young woman to giggle. The cat curled up and Shelly ran her hand over the silky fur.

In a few minutes, Shelly had fallen asleep and soon a dream began to form.

Shelly and her sister, Lauren, sat at the same table with the same women as in a previous dream. The twin sisters shared food and laughed along with the people at the table. Money rained down from the ceiling again, but no one paid any attention. The dollar bills formed into the cyclone and flew up and away.

Suddenly, Lauren's facial expression changed from happy and joyful to sad and sorrowful. Shelly tried to ask her what was wrong, but her sister couldn't hear what she was saying.

When Shelly lifted her wine glass to her lips, Lauren reached over and took it away from her. She put the glass to her own mouth and drained the contents, and then she turned the glass upside down and set it on the table.

A song started over the restaurant's speakers and it began with a drum solo.

Bang, bang, bang.

Shelly sat up, blinking. Justice stood on the back of the sofa looking at the front door. Someone was knocking.

Hurrying to the door, Shelly peeked out of the living room window as she passed and spotted Juliet on the front porch.

Opening the door, she said, "Sorry, I was napping. The knocking woke me."

Juliet entered the living room and sank into a chair. "I could use a nap, too. I'm beat." Justice jumped onto the young woman's lap and curled into a ball, ready to snooze.

Shelly brought her friend a cup of tea and a muffin.

Taking a bite of the toasted muffin, Juliet mumbled. "Did you dream when you were napping?"

Taking a seat on the sofa, Shelly pulled her legs up under her. "I did, but it wasn't very eventful." She related the dream to Juliet.

"Money fell from the ceiling, huh? What restaurant was this? Maybe we should go there tonight."

Shelly smiled. "It was only a dream, not a premonition. I don't think money will actually fall down on us."

"What does it mean?" Juliet sipped her tea and rested her legs on the ottoman.

"Your guess is as good as mine." Shelly pushed a few strands of hair from her eyes.

"Who was in the dream?"

Shelly thought about the people who had been sitting around the table. "I only recognized Emma Pinkley."

"Where was I sitting?" Juliet asked.

Shelly thought for a few moments, mentally recalling the faces around the table. "You weren't with us."

Juliet looked glum. "No? Where was I?"

"You weren't in the dream," Shelly told her.

"Well, why wasn't I? You said you were with your friends." Juliet sounded slightly indignant.

Juliet's words pinged in Shelly's head and a flash of anxiety raced through her, but she didn't know why. A puzzled look crossed over Shelly's face. "I ... I don't know."

9

J uliet joined Shelly for dinner to enjoy the vegetable soup that had been simmering in the slow cooker for most of the day. It was warm enough outside to open the sliding glass door in the kitchen and the two friends sat at the table in front of the doors while Justice settled on the floor in a patch of sunlight.

Lifting a spoonful of soup to her mouth, Juliet paused and said, "I'm going to have to have a talk with your subconscious. If you have dreams where you go out to do something with friends, then I have to be included. You can't leave me out."

Shelly pulled off a small hunk of her crusty bread. "When I think about the dream, the people around the table weren't really any of my friends.

They were people I hardly know, acquaintances from town, from the resort. Some I didn't even know at all. Why would my mind put me at a restaurant with them?"

"You'll have to ask your brain." Juliet slipped the spoon back into her bowl. "The soup is delicious."

"I saw Dwayne at the farm today. He's doing well, getting stronger every day. We talked about Emma Pinkley and the circumstances of her death."

"You mean her murder," Juliet said.

"Dwayne had something interesting to share."

Juliet looked up from her dinner and rested her spoon on the bread plate. "Tell me."

Shelly explained what Dwayne overheard while he was in the hospital.

"He's sure it was Charlie Pinkley he heard?"

"He says he's sure. He recognized Charlie's voice."

"And this happened within the last month." Juliet thought about the timing of Dwayne's hospitalization and Emma's murder. "It definitely could be Charlie who killed Emma. He was a suspect in our minds before Dwayne even told you what he heard."

"Why would Charlie think he could get away with such a thing?" Shelly asked. "He must be a smart guy. He made it through nursing school and training. In a murder investigation, the police often consider the husband or the family members first. How would Charlie think he could emerge from law enforcement's scrutiny unscathed?"

"Wishful thinking?" Juliet asked.

"Could be. The daughter, Aubrey, said her father went to the mall on the evening of the murder and didn't get home until around 10:30pm," Shelly said. "Was he really at the mall or was that his story?"

"He could have gone there for a short time and then left to ambush Emma somewhere," Juliet speculated. "The police must have gathered Emma's phone records. The records would indicate if Emma got a call or text from Charlie. He could have pretended car trouble and when his wife arrived to help him, he shot her."

"Charlie might have hired someone to do his dirty work," Shelly pointed out. "Maybe he really did stay at the mall until it closed. He'd be on the mall's security tapes. Those tapes would prove he was there and then he would have a rock-solid alibi for his whereabouts proving he did not kill Emma."

"Hmmm." Juliet said, "He may not have pulled the trigger, but he certainly could have planned it."

"Agreed."

Juliet said, "We're supposed to go with Jay

tomorrow afternoon to sit in on Charlie Pinkley's interview. It will give us a chance to watch him while he answers Jay's questions."

"I'm interested in how that will go and if we'll believe what he says," Shelly said.

"We might come away with a very different opinion of him than we have going in. We need to keep our minds open about him."

"Very true." Shelly told Juliet about Emma's friends. "Her daughter told us the names of several women who were friendly with Emma. I met one of them at the diner. Monica Jones, a park ranger."

"I know who she is. She's worked at the mountain for years. She's well thought of."

Shelly listed off the names of two other women and Juliet perked up when she heard Leena Tate's name.

"Leena runs the pastry café in town. She's there all the time. Let's go now and see if we can talk to her about Emma."

After cleaning up the dinner dishes, Shelly and Juliet walked into town and found a table in the High Rise Café and Bakery. Leena came out of the back room carrying a tray of sweets. The woman, in her mid-thirties, was tall and lean with her black hair pulled up in a ponytail. Leena took the young women's order and in a few minutes, carried the cups of tea and slices of chocolate cake to their table.

Juliet introduced themselves. "We heard you were a friend of Emma Pinkley. We were sorry to hear about your friend."

Leena looked surprised, but thanked them for their kind words. "I'd only met Emma a few months ago. I ran into her at the gym. We got along great. She was a really nice person."

"Would you like to sit down for a few minutes?" Shelly gestured to the table. "Would you mind talking with us about Emma?"

Leena glanced around the café and when she saw everything was being taken care of by her employee, she took a seat. "Were you friends of Emma?"

"We both work at the resort so we ran into her now and then," Juliet said. "Have you lived in town long?"

"About three years. I bought the café and made the move."

Shelly had planned to purchase a bakery in Boston, but the car accident put a stop to that. Being unable to work for months, Shelly had to live on the money she'd saved for her future store, and although she was grateful she'd had the money to draw from, it was a heartfelt disappointment to have to let go of owning the bakery she'd had her eye on. Shelly stifled a sad sigh. So much would be different if they hadn't been on the highway that day.

"Your shop is great," Shelly told Leena. "You did a nice job with the décor and the menu." She told the woman she was a baker and they talked about recipes, customer service, and how hard it was to get up so early in the morning for work until Shelly shifted the conversation back to Emma. "You met Emma at the gym?"

"We took some classes together and we'd meet to work out a couple of times a week."

"Did you get together with Emma and some of her other friends?" Juliet asked.

"Once in a while," Leena said. "Running the café swallows up my time. I don't get out as much as I'd like to. By dinnertime, I usually just want to go home and read or watch television."

"Did Emma seem worried about anything?"

Leena shook her head. "If she was worried about something, she hid it well."

"Had you met Emma's husband?" Shelly questioned.

"No, I hadn't. I did meet her daughter once when Aubrey came to the gym with Emma."

"Did Emma talk about her family?"

"She loved to talk about the kids." Leena smiled. "She sure was proud of them."

"Did she talk about Charlie?" Shelly asked.

"Sometimes. Nothing much, just what they'd been doing." Leena gave a shrug. "That's all. Mostly we talked about work, and working out, what we had planned for the weekend, things like that. Nothing monumental."

"Did Emma seem happy with Charlie?" Juliet asked.

One of Leena's eyebrows raised at the question. "I guess so. She didn't give any indication she wasn't. Why do you ask?"

"We heard there might be some marital issues," Juliet told her.

"I don't know about that. Sometimes, Emma complained about her husband, but it was minor annoyances like you'd have with anyone you lived with."

"Nothing major? No talk about breaking up?" Shelly asked.

"Never. Not to me anyway."

"When was the last time you saw Emma?"

Leena's shoulders hunched slightly. "The day she died."

Shelly and Juliet stared at the woman.

"You saw Emma that day?" Shelly asked as a flash of adrenaline raced through her. "Where?"

"I knew Emma went to her mother's house in Linville for dinner on Fridays and I asked her if she could drive me to a garage I use over there to service my car," Leena said. "I wanted to pick it up. It's not that convenient for me to take the car there, but the owner comes into the café almost every morning and I want to reciprocate by giving him my business."

"Emma picked you up and took you there?" Shelly asked.

"She did. She dropped me off at the garage."

"Did she tell you she was going to her mother's for dinner?"

"She said she had to change the dinner plans, but she was going to her mom's house anyway to drop off some food to her."

"Did Emma say why she had to change her plans?"

Leena thought for a few seconds. "I don't think she did. I don't remember her saying why. I don't know if it was Emma or her mother who had to change the plans."

"Did Emma give any indication what else she planned to do that night?" Shelly asked.

"I think she told me she had to do some errands and some shopping. She didn't say what the errands were."

"What road did you take to Linville?" Juliet asked.

Leena blinked a few times before answering, but then she told Juliet the route they took to get to the garage in Linville. "It was the most direct route. Why do you ask?"

"I wondered if Emma took the same way back to town that she took to Linville."

"I'm not sure. After she dropped me off, she left to go to her mother's place. I only saw her leave the parking lot and turn left onto the street. I have no idea what roads she took after that."

"Did she seem like herself that day? Was anything bothering her?" Shelly asked.

"She seemed a little quieter than usual, but that doesn't mean anything," Leena said. "She probably had a lot on her mind."

"Did she mention anyone's name while she was driving you to Linville?"

"I don't remember her talking about anyone except her mother and her daughter."

"She didn't mention a friend or a work colleague?"

"No one." Leena gave a shrug. "Oh, she did get a text right when we pulled into the garage's lot."

Shelly's senses started to buzz. "Do you know who texted Emma?"

"It was just her husband."

"Do you know what he wanted? What he texted her about?" Juliet's voice was tinged with anticipation.

"No. Emma glanced at the phone on the console. She said something like, *Charlie ... he'll just have to cool his jets.*"

Shelly and Juliet exchanged a look. *What did that mean?*

10

Emma Pinkley's husband, Charlie, age forty-four, was just under six feet tall, slim, with short blond hair and dark blue eyes. He sat in the small, cramped conference room in the police station with Jay and Shelly sitting opposite. Juliet was outside the room in a tiny booth watching through the one-way glass.

Charlie exuded a natural charm, but it was diminished by his slightly arrogant manner that mixed in with the outgoing personality. He sat back in his chair looking relaxed and at ease. Shelly could see how some people would find the man attractive. She saw a man who seemed oddly unaffected by his wife's recent murder.

"Thanks for coming in again," Jay said and then

explained Shelly's presence by telling the man the young woman helped out in the police station with different tasks such as taking notes during meetings and interviews.

"Can you tell us once more how you spent the late afternoon and evening on the day your wife passed away?" Jay asked.

Charlie gave the woman a smile and a nod. "I worked at the hospital and after my shift, I went home, showered, and had a bite to eat with my daughter. Later, I went to the Stockville mall to do some shopping."

"Did your daughter accompany you?" Jay asked.

"Aubrey wanted to get a jump on her weekend homework so she decided to stay home."

"Did you make any purchases at the mall?"

"I bought a pair of cowboy boots. I have the receipt if you need it to prove where I was."

"What time did you arrive at the mall?" Jay asked.

"I got there around 7pm." Anticipating the next question, Charlie said, "I left the mall around nine, stopped for gas. It was a pretty night. The moon was almost full. I got home a little after 10:30pm."

Shelly wrote notes on the laptop and glanced over at Jay who gave her a little nod indicating it was okay for Shelly to ask questions. "Did you try the shoe store on Main Street in the center of town? They have a great selection of boots, some are hand-made and others are one-of-a-kind."

Charlie studied Shelly for a moment. "I looked there. I didn't find anything I liked so I decided to try the mall."

"Would you mind bringing in the receipt for the boots?" Shelly asked. "It's simply protocol. I need to log it into the case notes." It *wasn't* protocol, but Shelly wanted to have a look at the receipt.

Charlie leaned to the side and removed his wallet from his back pocket. "I have it right here." He tossed the receipt onto the table and slid it over to Jay.

"Thank you." Jay asked, "Where were you when you found out about your wife's death?"

"I was at home. An officer came to the door. I went to the hospital. The kids came, too. Emma had already passed when we got there."

"There are some delicate questions that have to be asked," Jay said. "I understand it can be difficult to discuss personal aspects of our lives, but it is necessary in cases like this."

Charlie's face tightened.

"It's come to our attention that you have had some issues with gambling."

"I knew that would come up." Charlie tried to keep the defensive tone out of his voice. "It hasn't been a problem lately."

"When was the last time there was a problem?" Jay asked.

Charlie exhaled. "About six months ago."

"And was there a problem prior to that?"

"About a year and a half ago."

"Some debts accumulated from the gambling?" Jay questioned.

"Yeah. Emma told me I should go to counseling to get help."

"Did you go?"

"Not the first time I gambled, but I did go a few months ago."

"Are you still working with the counselor?" Jay asked.

"I went a few times, but we didn't hit off. I was trying to find someone I liked better."

"Did you find the counseling helpful?"

Charlie shrugged. "Not really."

Jay asked, "How were you and Emma able to pay off the debt?"

A little color rose up Charlie's neck. Shelly

guessed it was probably more from annoyance with the question than from any feelings of embarrassment or guilt. "We had savings so we used that the first time. The second time, we took a home equity loan to pay for some of it. Emma got a part-time job for a while to pay off the rest."

"Was that at Windsor Manufacturing?" Jay questioned.

"Yes, it was."

"How did Emma like working there?"

"She liked it well-enough. It was only a temporary thing."

"Did you pick up any extra shifts at the hospital to help pay off the debts?" Jay asked.

"I couldn't. There weren't any available shifts."

"In the weeks leading up to the crime, did Emma seem herself?" Jay asked the man.

"I thought she did."

"No signs of worry or anxiety? No arguments with anyone?"

"Nothing like that. Not that I know of."

"Did she indicate any concerns for her safety?" Jay questioned.

"Not to me she didn't."

"Would you say you and Emma had a close relationship?"

Charlie's mouth turned up in a slight grin. "We were married, so yeah."

"Did you consider Emma your best friend?"

"Uh. I guess you could say that. I have guy friends, too."

Jay looked squarely at the man. "Did Emma have a life insurance policy?"

Charlie's eyes darted around the room. "Yeah, she did. I did, too."

"And how much was that policy for?"

Charlie squirmed a little in his seat. "Five-hundred thousand dollars."

"When was that taken out?"

"About six months ago."

A cold shiver ran over Shelly's skin.

"We both got policies. In case something happened." Charlie swallowed and his Adam's apple moved up and down in his throat. "We wanted the kids to be okay if anything happened to one of us."

"Please forgive this next question," Jay said. "Have you ever been unfaithful to your wife?"

Charlie's jaw moved like he was clenching his teeth together and he leaned forward with both arms on the table. "Look, I know people talk. I like to go out, have a few drinks. Sometimes, I flirt. So what? It's just good fun. I always go back home to Emma and the kids."

"So you have never been unfaithful?" Jay pressed.

"Listen, I'm a good guy. I like to go out and have some fun. Who doesn't? It doesn't mean anything. It's just flirting."

"Have you ever had an affair?" Jay reworded her question.

"Come on. I was married to Emma."

"That doesn't answer the question, Mr. Pinkley," Jay said with stern eyes.

Charlie rubbed his face. "Yeah, okay. I hung out with some women over the years. None of it ever meant anything."

"Were you in a *relationship* with any of the women?"

"No, for Pete's sake. I flirted. I had a few flings. It was never anything serious with anyone. I always went home to Emma."

Shelly wanted to roll her eyes.

"When was the last time you had a *fling*?" Jay asked the man using his own word to describe his indiscretion.

Charlie looked down at the table. "I don't know. Maybe six months ago."

"Can you tell us the woman's name?"

Charlie made eye contact with Jay, his expression angry. "No, I can't. I don't remember her name. It was one night. One night."

"There may come a point in the investigation into your wife's death when it may be important to know the name of some of the women you've been with," Jay informed Charlie. "It might be a good idea over the next few days to try to refresh your memory." Jay glanced at her notes. "Did you call your wife on the afternoon or evening of her death?"

"I don't think so. I was busy at the hospital in the afternoon. When I was getting ready to head to the mall, I couldn't find my phone."

Jay looked up from her laptop and moved her gaze to Charlie. "Did you text her?"

"I don't think I texted her from work and I didn't have my phone with me when I went inside to shop."

"You didn't text Emma after you left home that evening?" Jay asked.

"I didn't have my phone so I couldn't send her a text," Charlie said with an edge to his voice.

When Jay was finished with a few minor questions, she thanked Charlie for coming in and showed him to the door. Juliet came in from the observation booth and closed the door behind her before taking a seat at the table next to Shelly.

"He's a real winner, isn't he?" Juliet asked with a groan. "He has *fun*, a few *flings*. He thinks those explanations absolve him from calling it 'cheating on his wife'."

"His definition of cheating is obviously different from ours." Jay opened her laptop and made a few notes.

"Emma had a life insurance policy. She got it six months ago," Shelly said. "A lot went on over the last six months, didn't it? Emma and Charlie took out substantial life insurance policies. Charlie had a 'fling' six months ago. Charlie incurred heavy amounts of debt from gambling six months ago."

"We'll look into all of his claims from that time," Jay said with narrowed eyes. "He says he can't remember the woman's name he was with six months ago. Charlie seems to be forgetful, or have some problems with his memory. We'll look into when he actually incurred the gambling debt, when he went to the counselor and for how long, when the life policies were taken out, and when the debt was paid off." Jay frowned. "Just in case Charlie isn't remembering those details correctly."

Shelly said, "Charlie didn't have his phone with

him when he went to the mall, and he denies texting Emma when he was on the way there. Leena Tate said a text came in when Emma was dropping her off at the auto repair garage. Leena told us Emma said *Charlie* in reference to him being the sender of the text."

Jay said, "We'll go through the phone company records. See if he's telling the truth or not."

Juliet looked at her friend and asked, "Why did you ask Charlie for the store receipt for his boots?"

"I wanted to see what he bought and I want to go to the leather store in town to see if they carry the boots Charlie bought at the mall." Shelly tilted her head. "Why drive an hour away if you can get what you want here in town?"

"And if the store in Paxton Park *does* carry those boots," Juliet said, "the answer to why Charlie drove all that way to the mall might be very interesting to hear."

11

Shelly and Juliet browsed the busy leather shop in the center of town looking for the brand and style of men's cowboy boots Charlie Pinkley had purchased at the mall.

"Here they are." Juliet said softly as she picked up a boot from one of the display tables and turned it over to look at the sole. "These are the same price as the boots from the mall."

"So it wasn't a higher price here that made him shop elsewhere," Shelly said. "Maybe they don't have his size here."

"What size was printed on the receipt?"

"Eleven and a half."

"I'll ask one of the sales clerks if they have them in that size." Juliet went to ask about the boots. In a few minutes, she was back. "They have them in stock. I told the woman I was thinking of buying them for a relative and wanted to check on the sizes available. She told me they have them in stock in every size from ten to twelve including half-sizes."

"So why go out of his way to buy these boots at the mall?" Shelly asked.

"Maybe we should visit the store where Charlie got them," Juliet suggested, putting the boots back on the table and moving to look at the shelves of women's shoes.

"I wonder if we should talk to Emma's mother and sister again?" Shelly wondered out loud.

A woman said, "Are you talking about Emma Pinkley?"

The two friends turned around to see one of the sales clerks standing behind them. Her name tag said *Dawn B*. In her mid-thirties, the woman was petite and attractive with blond hair to her shoulders, and blue eyes with long fake lashes.

"Were you friends of Emma?" Dawn asked.

"We were colleagues of Emma," Juliet explained. "We work at the resort."

"Did you know Emma?" Shelly asked the woman.

"Yes. She was a friend of mine. Such a wonderful

person." Dawn shook her head sadly. "Why would someone shoot her? I just can't wrap my head around it."

"How did you know Emma?"

"I met her through a mutual acquaintance. We took an exercise class together. We weren't best friends, but we'd get together sometimes for dinner or lunch or to go shopping."

"We only knew her casually," Shelly told the woman. "She seemed like a nice person."

"Do you know her family?" Juliet asked.

"I met her kids a couple of times," Dawn said brushing at her eyes. "I hope they're doing okay."

Juliet asked, "How about her husband? Do you know him?"

"I met him once. He must be devastated. Have you heard if there'll be a service for Emma?" Dawn asked.

"We haven't, no. Maybe the family is planning something private." Shelly asked, "When did you see Emma last?"

"Oh, let's see. A group of us went out for dinner together. That must have been about three weeks ago. I ran into Emma at the coffee shop about a week ago. We sat together for a little while to chat." Dawn put her hand on her chest and let out a sad sigh.

"Did Emma seem worried about anything when you saw her at the coffee shop?" Shelly questioned.

"She seemed fine. Her usual self."

"Did she complain about anything?"

"No, she was in a good mood, she was happy." Dawn noticed one of the customers holding a shoe from the shelf. "I'd better get back to work. Nice talking to you. Let me know if I can get your size if you want to try anything on."

When the woman was out of ear shot, Shelly said, "Emma's daughter didn't mention her mother had a friend named Dawn."

Juliet shrugged. "Kids don't know all their parents' friends. Dawn said she and Emma weren't best friends. Maybe the daughter didn't think of Dawn."

"Maybe," Shelly said. "I'd like to talk to Emma's mother again. I'll ask Jay about it."

JAY DROVE the car to Emma's mother's house with Juliet in the front passenger seat and Shelly sitting in the back watching the tall trees flash by as they rode along the country lanes. Whenever she traveled by car, Shelly became tense and anxious recalling the accident she was in on the Boston highway. When she could, she avoided riding in autos and preferred to get around Paxton Park on her bicycle. She hadn't yet experienced winter in the mountain resort and knew that the bike would not be adequate transportation for her during the snowy months. For now, she didn't want to think about possibly needing a car.

Emma's mother, Nancy, welcomed the women into her home. "Is there some news to tell me?" she asked hopefully.

"I'm afraid not," Jay spoke softly. "We're working hard on the case."

When everyone was settled on the chairs and the sofa of the living room, Jay said, "We'd like to talk more with you about Emma. Can you tell us who some of her friends were?"

Nancy's hands were clasped together in her lap. "There's Monica, Monica Jones. She's a park ranger at the mountain. And there's Peggy Lane, she works at the law firm on Main Street. Oh, let's see. Emma mentioned a woman named Leena who she met at the gym. They'd been getting together every once in a while. Emma didn't have a lot of friends, what with working full time and running the household and taking care of the kids. She didn't have much free time. Emma met Monica when they were middle school kids. They've been friends for a long time."

Shelly asked, "Do you know someone named Dawn? Her last name begins with a 'B.' She's in her mid-thirties, blond, petite. We believe she was friendly with Emma."

Nancy's eyebrows pinched together in thought. "Oh, do you mean Dawn Barry?"

"That must be her. She works in the leather shop in town?"

"Emma told me Dawn works there." Nancy gave a nod.

"Dawn and Emma were friends?" Jay asked.

"Well, I guess you could say *friendly*." Nancy shrugged. "Emma didn't really like Dawn. It's okay for me to tell you how Emma felt. You won't spread it around."

"How did Emma feel about Dawn?" Juliet asked.

"Dawn was draining. She'd talk your ear off, all about herself, of course. That's what Emma told me. I never met the woman. I think they met at the gym or maybe, through someone they both knew. Anyway, Emma didn't really want a friendship with Dawn, but if Dawn called to go shopping or something, Emma felt she should go."

"Why did she feel obliged to go?" Shelly asked.

"Emma wasn't sure if Dawn had many friends. She said she didn't want to hurt Dawn's feelings, so she usually went along when she was asked to do something. Why are you asking about Emma's friends?"

"We try to talk to as many people as possible," Jay explained. "To get a good picture of the person's life, daily habits. We can learn a good deal from friends, family, work associates."

Nancy nodded.

"When we were here earlier, you told us you didn't trust your son-in-law, that you didn't like him," Jay said. "Can you tell us why?"

Nancy's eyes moved around the room and she twisted her hands. "It's just a feeling."

"Is it based on anything in particular?" Jay asked.

Nancy's expression hardened. "The stupid gambling, for one thing. Getting the family into so much debt. Twice, he did that. Twice. Charlie only thinks about himself, want he wants, what he needs. He never looks beyond the end of his nose. He's a selfish, self-centered man."

"Did Emma say these things to you?" Shelly asked.

"She didn't come right out and say them. Emma was too nice, too forgiving." Nancy had to swallow hard to remove the emotion that was starting to choke her. "She should have divorced Charlie. He was good for nothing. She didn't need that albatross around her neck."

"Did Emma ever talk to you about divorcing him?" Jay asked.

"A couple of times when she was fed up with his antics. I doubt she would have gone through with it," Nancy said. "She hated conflict."

"How do you and Charlie get along?" Jay questioned. "When you're together, do you manage to get along with each other?"

"I'm civil, friendly. Even though I don't feel like being that way. Charlie acts like everything is fine. We don't argue or ignore each other. I'm cordial to him for the kids' sakes."

"Did you see any cracks in the marriage? From Charlie's point of view?"

"Do you mean did he want to get out of the marriage?" Nancy asked. "I don't see why he would. Emma brought in a good salary. She ran the house, made a nice home, took care of everything, raised the kids to be good people. She did a lot to pay off Charlie's gambling debts. Why would he want out of that? Emma did all the work and Charlie reaped all the benefits."

"Did you know Emma and Charlie recently took out life insurance policies?" Jay asked.

"Emma told me. I was glad she'd get some money if something ever happened to Charlie."

"Do you think Charlie ever cheated on Emma?"

Nancy made a face. "Charlie did cheat. Emma figured it out. Charlie liked to go out drinking. A few people told Emma about Charlie's behavior in the bars, that he left with a woman some times."

"Did Emma confront Charlie about it?" Shelly asked.

"I'm not sure. Emma tried to look the other way, but sometimes she would be plenty angry about it," Nancy said. "Why couldn't Charlie just be happy with his family? He caused Emma a lot of heartbreak."

"Do you know what Emma's plans were on the night the crime took place?" Jay asked.

"I don't know. She only said she had a lot to do and would like to postpone dinner until the next night." Nancy squeezed her hands together. "I should have asked what she was doing. I should have asked more questions. I should have made her stay for dinner." A few tears rolled down the woman's face.

"It's okay." Jay spoke kindly. "We have all our

resources working on the case. We'll figure it out. I'll do everything in my power to find the person responsible."

Nancy gave a nod and then buried her face in her hands.

12

It was a cool, sunny morning when Shelly and Jay arrived at Windsor Manufacturing, the company where Emma Pinkley had worked part-time for several months. Phone records indicated that a man who worked at Windsor, Steve Carlton, had made many calls and sent numerous texts to Emma during the time she worked there. Jay had a specific interest in Carlton and had arranged to speak with him in the company office.

A conference room had been set aside by the president of Windsor for Jay to do the interview, and Carlton was the first person she and Shelly would meet with.

Steve Carlton was tall, with a medium build, dark brown hair and brown eyes. He wore slacks, a well-pressed shirt, and a navy blazer. A few beads of perspiration showed on the man's upper lip and when he shook hands with Shelly, his palm felt damp.

"Thanks for speaking with us," Jay told the man. "What do you do here at Windsor?"

Carlton cleared his throat. "I'm an assistant vice president. I oversee the financial side of things."

"Where do you live?"

"I live here in Rollingwood. About a ten-minute drive away."

"Are you married? Do you have a family?" Jay asked.

"I'm married. We have two kids, two boys. They're eighteen and sixteen."

"Does your wife work?"

"She's a teacher at the middle school."

"You knew Emma Pinkley?" Jay asked.

"Yes, Emma worked here for a few months in the accounting department. She was a good employee, smart, hard-working."

Shelly watched the man over the top of the laptop screen and noted his slightly twitchy behavior, pulling at his sleeve, adjusting his blazer, shifting around a little in his chair. His forehead glistened with a thin layer of sweat.

"Did you interact much with Mrs. Pinkley?" Jay asked.

"Some. She was only part-time, as I said."

"When you talked with her, did she appear worried about anything?"

"No, she didn't. I only knew her for a short time. The position was temporary. I didn't know her well so I wouldn't have picked up on whether or not she was bothered by anything."

Shelly narrowed her eyes at the man as she typed the notes.

"Was Emma friendly with anyone in the office?"

"I'm not sure. I didn't notice."

"Did you ever socialize with Emma?"

"Me? No, I didn't."

"Did you ever go to Paxton Park to see her?"

"Well, no. Why would I do that?"

"I wondered that myself," Jay said with a stern tone.

Carlton looked nervously around the room. "What do you mean?"

Shelly was pretty sure Carlton knew very well what Jay was talking about.

"Cell phone records show quite a few calls and texts from your phone to Emma's phone." Jay let the words hang in the air.

Carlton sat straighter, his face expressionless. "I got in touch to ask questions about what she was working on, to clarify information. She wasn't here every day so I needed to contact her for business reasons."

"I see." Jay opened a folder and shuffled some papers. "Most of the calls went unanswered and Emma only replied to one of your texts." Jay looked up. "Why wouldn't Emma answer your calls?"

Carlton's jaw twitched. "I don't know."

"Did you ask her why she didn't answer them?"

"I don't recall asking her about that."

Jay looked down at one of the papers and then clasped her hands over her folder. "We heard some information about what you had texted Emma. My guess is that Emma did not appreciate your suggestive, lewd, and inappropriate messages and chose not to answer your calls or your texts. What do you say to that?"

Carlton's lips were held tightly together.

"The records also indicate that your phone was in the vicinity of Emma Pinkley's neighborhood about two weeks prior to her death." Jay's eyes were like lasers.

Carlton raised his voice. "I didn't have anything to do with her death. Do I need a lawyer?"

"You are welcome to retain an attorney if you choose to, Mr. Carlton, but we are not charging you with anything," Jay said. "We are simply gathering information. Now, would you like to explain your behavior with the calls and texts?"

Carlton's cheeks colored pink. "I thought Emma was attractive. I thought she was attracted to me. I asked her out a few times, just to have dinner. One afternoon, I had business in Paxton Park and drove over to her house. She wasn't at home. No one was at the house. It was only a friendly call. I just stopped by to say hello."

"I might infer that Emma did not want the attention you were giving her. Would I be correct in that?"

"I was only being friendly," Carlton's tone was defensive.

"I might call it something else," Jay stared at the man.

Carlton squirmed in his seat.

"You told me at the beginning of the interview that you are married. Did I hear that correctly?"

"Yes, you did." Carlton's voice was softer.

"And Emma was married as well."

"Yes."

Jay let out a long breath. "I'm concerned that you

don't seem to understand boundaries. How far would you push boundaries, Mr. Carlton?"

"I ... what do you mean?" Carlton said with forced indignation.

"Where were you on the evening that Emma Pinkley died?"

A shiver went down Shelly's back as she waited for the man's reply.

"I was at home."

"Was anyone at home with you?"

"My wife arrived home around 10pm."

"And your sons?"

"They were on an overnight school trip."

"So you were alone in the house until 10pm?" Jay asked.

"That's right."

"Did you leave the house for any reason between six and ten?"

"I did not. I was at home the entire evening."

"Did anyone see you at home? A neighbor? A friend? A relative?"

"No. I was inside the house working in my office."

"Did it bother you that Emma did not return your interest?" Jay questioned.

"No," Carlton said a little too forcefully. "I mean,

sure, I would have liked to have been friends outside of work, but Emma was a busy woman. That's understandable. There were no hard feelings."

Shelly was amazed at Carlton's ability to make it seem his only intention was to be friends with Emma. She had to stop herself from making a face and shaking her head at the man's comments.

"When was the last time you saw Emma?" Jay asked.

"Her last day here at Windsor. I don't remember the exact date."

"And when was the last time you talked to her?"

"The same day. Her last day here at work."

"When was the last time you attempted to speak with her?"

"I don't know." Carlton's muscles tightened along his jaw line as he glanced at Jay's folder. "You can probably tell me since you have the records. I called to see how she was doing. I don't recall what day it was. That's all it was. A friendly call."

Jay asked several more questions and then thanked Steve Carlton for speaking with them. The man stood up, nodded, and left the room without saying goodbye or shaking their hands.

"That was an abrupt ending to the meeting."

Shelly closed the laptop. "I don't think he enjoyed our company," she said with a sly look at Jay.

"He got caught. I'm always baffled when smart people do stupid things. Carlton must know that the phone companies have records of calls, their duration, whether or not the call was answered." Jay sighed and shook her head. "He must know that cell towers and cell phones ping each other and that those pings can be used to narrow down a location and indicate where a phone has been."

"I guess people get lazy. Or their desires make them forget that it's hard to hide from technology." Shelly slipped her laptop into its case. "What do you think? Is Carlton a person of interest?"

"The records tell us that Carlton's phone was in Rollingwood on the night Emma was killed," Jay said. "But just because Carlton's phone was in Rollingwood, it doesn't mean that Carlton was."

As Jay packed up her laptop and folders, a knock on the open door caused her to look up.

A young woman in her late twenties stood in the hallway looking in. "Excuse me. Do you have a minute to talk?"

"Come in," Shelly said with a smile. "How can we help?"

The petite woman had sandy blond hair pulled

up in a loose bun. She stepped slowly into the room, but gave the impression she might dart away before saying another word. "Can I shut the door?"

"Yes, please." Shelly sat down in order to reassure the young woman and then introduced herself and Jay.

"I'm Linden Parker. I work in the accounting department."

"You knew Emma Pinkley?"

"I did." Linden sat down at the table and pushed nervously at her bangs. "I heard you were talking to some of the employees." She took a quick look at the door and Shelly thought she might bolt.

"Did you want to tell us something?" Jay asked gently.

"I liked Emma. She was a really nice person." Linden wrung her hands together. "Emma was smart. She did a great job. But I think some people were jealous of her. Some people weren't that nice to her."

"How do you mean?" Shelly asked.

"Unfriendly. Unhelpful. You know when you start a new job, you have questions and it's nice to have someone you can ask things. One of the other accountants was rude, she wouldn't answer Emma's questions. She even gave her wrong information. I helped when I could, whenever it was something I knew."

"Is that what you wanted to tell us?" Jay asked.

Linden took another glance at the door. "No. I'm babbling. You were talking to Steve?"

"We did, yes." Shelly gave a nod.

"I just want you to know, I'm not accusing anyone of anything," Linden said softly.

Shelly and Jay gave the woman time to say what she needed to.

"The day Emma died." Linden took a deep breath. "It was early evening. I was out to dinner with my boyfriend. We were in Paxton Park, near Linville. We had a table on the outside patio. They had those tall metal heaters going. It was nice. I saw Emma's car drive past. I knew it was her car because she has that little ball of the world on top of her antenna. A few minutes later, I saw Steve Carlton drive by."

"You know his car?" Jay asked.

"I do. It's a convertible. Blue. It has a sticker on the window for parking in the lot here. It's orange with a triangle. It was Steve."

"Could you see if he was alone?" Shelly asked.

"I'm not sure, but I think so. The top was up, but I'm pretty sure there wasn't anyone in the passenger seat. I thought maybe Emma and Steve were heading somewhere together, with Steve following her, but I know Emma didn't like him so I was confused."

"Did Emma have someone in the car with her?"

"Yes. Another woman. She had dark hair." Linden stared down at the table. "When I heard what happened to Emma, I.... well, I ... I'm not accusing Steve. I just thought ... I thought I should tell someone what I saw." The young woman stood up abruptly. "I need to get back to my desk now. Sorry to take up your time."

As soon as Linden was gone, Shelly and Jay exchanged worried looks.

"So Steve Carlton was in Paxton Park shortly before Emma was shot," Jay said.

A sinking feeling filled Shelly's chest.

13

Shelly rode in the front passenger seat of Jack's SUV. Every once in a while, she gripped the console or the grab-bar on the door. Jack was used to his girlfriend's dramatic reaction to twists and turns on the winding country roads and knowing her behavior was due to lingering anxiety over the car accident, he never called attention to it.

Jack was driving the roads Emma would have taken on the night she was murdered so that they could get a sense of where she was, and when she was there.

"The automotive garage should be up ahead on the left," Jack said. "The road we took from town is the most likely way Emma took to drop off her friend, Leena, at the garage. It wouldn't make any sense to pick up Leena in town and then drive a different route. This was the most direct way to go."

"This is the way Leena told us she went with Emma." When Shelly grasped the dashboard with both hands as Jack turned into the garage's parking lot, she gave the man a sheepish look. "Sorry. It's not your driving."

Jack gave her a reassuring smile. "I know what it is. It's okay." He joked with her when he added, "I've learned it's best to ignore you when you're riding in the car."

"Smart man." Shelly nodded. "So this is the place where Leena gets her car serviced and where Emma dropped her off that evening. I assume Emma left here and went to her mother's house a couple of miles down the road."

"Want to drive there?" Jack asked.

"Yeah, let's see how long it takes." Shelly gave Jack the address and he punched it into the GPS for directions.

When he was about to turn right, Shelly asked him to stop. "Wait a minute." She leaned forward to better see the lit-up map on the dash. "The directions are telling you to go right, but I distinctly recall

Leena telling me she watched Emma leave the lot and turn to the left."

"The directions aren't always perfect. Does it look like we should turn left?"

"No, it doesn't. Turning right is the way to Emma's mother's house." Shelly lifted her eyes from the map to look at Jack. "Why did she go left?"

"Let's follow the road and have a look."

They drove along the quiet roads with the forest on both sides.

"If we keep going, this will take us to the other side of the mountain. What time did Emma's mother say she got to her house?" Jack asked.

"Emma got to her mom's place around 7pm. Leena said she got dropped off around 6:30pm."

"It would take ten minutes to drive from the garage to the mother's house," Jack said. "Where did Emma go? There haven't been any roads leading off of this one. If she drove too far in this direction, Emma wouldn't have had the time to get back to her mother's home by 7pm. The longest she could have driven in this direction would have been ten minutes."

Shelly said, "Ten minutes along this road, ten minutes back to the garage, and then ten minutes to get to her mom's."

"We've already gone ten minutes in this direction and there haven't been any stores or restaurants or anything for Emma to stop at," Jack said pulling his vehicle to the side of the road. "What do you think?"

"Did Emma notice that Steve Carlton was following her?" Shelly asked. "Did she spot him and drive out of the garage lot to the left? Maybe she didn't want him following her to her mom's house. Maybe she drove a little way up the road and when she saw he was still tailing her, she pulled over to tell Steve to get lost."

"That could very well be what happened." Jack shifted in his seat to face Shelly. "Emma probably didn't want Steve to get anywhere near her mother's place. I'll bet she didn't want the guy to know where her mother lived."

A frown pulled at Shelly's mouth. "Now what? Where did Emma go after she left her mom's house? Her mother told us Emma left about fifteen minutes after arriving, so around 7:15pm. The medical examiner said Emma could have driven from Linville, Rollingwood, or West Rollingwood after being shot and still could have made it to the center of Paxton Park." Shelly rubbed at her chin. "But, I think that's an ambitious idea."

Jack gave his girlfriend a questioning look.

"If I got shot, I would be panicked. Maybe I would try to drive back to town to get help. Maybe I wouldn't want to stop to call for help because the shooter was following after me. I'm losing blood. I'm getting weaker. How far could I really go under those conditions without crashing the car? I'd be driving fast at first, but I bet I'd start to slow the car because I was getting dizzy and weak. Maybe it would be possible for someone to drive from those three towns based solely on the science of how long it would take for the blood loss to cause you to blackout, but there are other considerations, like panic, becoming woozy, maybe getting disoriented, definitely weakening. Could Emma have really been that far away from where she crashed?" Shaking her head, Shelly said, "I don't think so."

Jack drove back the way they'd come and pulled into a restaurant's parking lot so they could get some dinner.

"This must be the restaurant that the woman from Windsor Manufacturing was having dinner when she noticed Emma and Steve Carlton drive by." Shelly got out of the car, headed to the heated patio area of tables, and turned around to look to the road. "It's a clear view of the passing cars."

Shelly and Jack were seated inside near a lit fireplace and the warmth lent the place a cozy atmosphere.

After the waiter took their orders and brought over the drinks, Jack said, "So this Steve Carlton should be on the suspect list. He harassed Emma with suggestive texts and made calls to her when she wasn't working at Windsor. The young woman from Windsor claims to have seen Steve driving a few minutes behind Emma when she was bringing Leena to the automotive place."

Shelly took a sip of her drink and set it down, alarm washing over her face. "Did Emma confront Steve after she dropped off Leena? Did she and Steve argue? Did Steve become angry? Did he continue to follow Emma after arguing with her?" Shelly took in a deep breath. "Is Steve the shooter?"

"It makes sense. It's possible." Jack moved his chair closer to Shelly and took her hand. "What about the husband, Charlie? He drank, gambled, went out with other women. When he was in the hospital, Dwayne from the orchard claims he heard Charlie say he wanted out of the marriage."

Shelly said, "And Charlie drove an hour to the mall to buy cowboy boots that were available in town at the same price."

"It seems we have two people on the suspect list," Jack said. "Is there anyone else?"

Shelly thought about the interviews she'd sat in on trying to recall the details of what was said at the meetings and how the interviewees behaved. Some small things tried to surface in her mind, but before she could grasp their importance they flickered away.

The two recent dreams she'd had where Lauren was present came to the forefront of her thoughts. Was her sister attempting to point her towards something? The situation in the dream was fairly mundane, some friends in a restaurant enjoying a meal and some drinks together. Except for the strange part where the money drifted down from the ceiling and then swirled together, shot up, and disappeared, the rest of the interaction in the dream was nothing out of the ordinary.

"Would you like another glass of wine?" Jack asked.

"No, thank you," Shelly said. The question about more wine made her remember that in the second dream, Lauren took Shelly's wine glass, drank the liquid, and then turned the glass upside down on the table. Odd. Why would she do that? Lauren's expression was sad when she took the glass away.

Why? What did it have to do with Emma Pinkley? Maybe it had nothing to do with the dead woman.

"Shelly?"

Shelly blinked and came out of her thoughts. "I was thinking over the conversations and the meetings I've had recently. I don't know. Charlie and Steve have to be considered suspects, but who else is there? It might have been someone Emma didn't know. She could have crossed paths with someone who was waiting for a victim. The shooting might have been random."

"It may have been someone random," Jack agreed, "but aren't most crimes against women committed by someone the victim knows?"

"I think that's right," Shelly nodded. "I feel like I'm missing things that are right under my nose and then I feel like I don't have access to all the puzzle pieces."

"This case is definitely a puzzle," Jack said. "A well-liked, respected woman from town is killed and no one can believe that the kind, caring Emma was shot by someone ... except there are two people to consider as possible suspects. Could there be others?"

The dreams ... Lauren ... friends around a table...

the overturned glass. What are the clues trying to tell me?

What do you do when you're putting together a puzzle and you don't have all the pieces?

You go and look for them.

14

"Shelly?" Melody called into the back workroom from the doorway to the front of the diner. "Monica is here."

"Thanks. I'm coming." Shelly hurried and slipped four loaves of bread into the ovens to bake and asked Henry to take them out if she wasn't back in time. She wanted to speak to Emma's friend, the park ranger, but Monica hadn't come into the diner for a few days.

Wiping her hands on her apron, Shelly went out front and found Monica sitting in the same booth where she'd talked with her previously. "Can I sit with you for a few minutes?"

Monica didn't look particularly happy about it, but she gave a curt nod.

"You haven't been in for a few days," Shelly started off the conversation.

"I'm feeling awful about Emma," Monica said rubbing at her eyes with her hand. "I haven't been sleeping. I miss her."

"I'm very sorry."

"I'm not good company right now. It isn't you. I'm sorry about seeming so unfriendly. I'm a mess over Emma's death."

Shelly murmured that she understood completely. "Would you mind if I run some things by you?"

"Like what?" Monica picked at the eggs on her plate.

"Sometimes, I work with the police on a part time basis. I go to interviews, take notes, do some research for them." Shelly didn't give the real reason she was present at meetings or interviews. Talking about her strong intuition seemed like a good way to scare people off so she didn't bring it up.

Monica raised her eyes to Shelly, wanting to hear more.

"Did Emma talk to you about a guy at Windsor Manufacturing? His name is Steve Carlton."

Monica's eyes darkened and her jaw tightened before she spoke. "I've heard all about Steve."

"Nothing good, I assume," Shelly said.

With a sigh, Monica said, "You'd assume correctly. Steve fell for Emma. He couldn't stand hearing the word no. It seemed to make him frantic ... frantic in his attempts to win over Emma." She shook her head. "I don't think Steve is ... normal. Emma was married, Steve is married, it didn't matter. His eye landed on Emma and he couldn't see anything else. He called her all the time. He texted her. It creeped me out."

"How did Emma handle it?"

"She wouldn't answer his calls. She ignored his texts. She made sure people were around when he wanted to talk to her at work. She wouldn't go to a conference room with him alone."

"Was Emma falling apart over what was happening?"

"At first, she was shocked. She couldn't believe it. This was stuff you read about or see in a movie, it doesn't happen to you," Monica said. "Emma behaved as a complete professional. She didn't smile, laugh, or joke around with Steve. She wouldn't even converse casually with him. It was all business, all the time. She was pretty bothered by Steve initially, but she wouldn't let it drive her out of Windsor. It was the best paying job she could get part time and she wanted the money to pay off those terrible gambling debts. She wouldn't quit."

"Emma must have talked to you a lot about the situation."

"She did."

"Did she tell anyone else what was happening?"

"No, just me. Well, I think she mentioned it to her mother, but she downplayed it. Emma needed someone to talk it out with. Really? She should have gone to the police about Steve's harassment."

"Did you give Emma advice?" Shelly asked.

"I sure did. I told her to quit the stupid job and get as far away from that creep as possible."

"What did Emma say to that?"

"She didn't agree with me. Emma got pepper spray to use on Steve if he happened to get any ideas." Monica took a swallow of her coffee. "Emma said that it didn't matter if she worked there or if she left the job. Steve would keep calling and texting. She even saw him driving around her neighborhood once. Emma told me he was obsessed with her and it wouldn't matter if she quit or not. So she didn't quit. She stuck it out for the money so she could get her family out of debt."

"Did Emma sway you to her side of it? Did she

convince you that staying at the job was an okay idea?"

"No. I kept telling her to get out of that job. I thought Steve would give up on her sooner if he wasn't seeing her in the office every day," Monica said.

"Why didn't you tell me about Steve before?" Shelly asked.

"You aren't a police officer or a detective." Monica gave a shrug. "What would be the point of me telling you this stuff. There isn't anything you can do about it. There wasn't any use in telling you."

"Did you ever meet Steve?"

"Thankfully, no."

Shelly leaned forward and kept her voice soft. "Do you think Steve could have had something to do with Emma getting shot?"

Monica's expression turned hard. "I wouldn't be at all surprised."

Shelly looked out the window at the lake and the mountains rising above the forest. She could almost smell the pine trees even though the windows were closed. How she wished she was outside in the sunshine hiking or biking on the mountain trails, far away from crime and murder and loss.

Turning back to Monica with a sigh, Shelly said,

"Emma's daughter, Aubrey, talked with me not long ago. She mentioned that Emma went out for dinner with some friends to celebrate leaving Windsor. Did you go?"

"I was supposed to go. It started out as a dinner with Emma, me, and Peggy going out together, but other people heard about it and sort of invited themselves."

"You didn't go?" Shelly asked.

"No. At the last minute, I was asked to take someone's place and attend a conference in Stockbridge so I couldn't make the dinner. Peggy couldn't go either. She has a four-month-old son and he came down with a bad cold and she couldn't leave him."

"Who ended up going to the dinner? Do you know?"

"Leena Tate went. Two people from the resort accounting department went. Dawn Barry went along, too. It started with only the three of us planning to go out, but it ended up for Emma being dinner with acquaintances, not with her two best friends."

Something about what Monica said picked at Shelly. "I heard Emma came home feeling sick with the flu."

"Yeah, she was in bad shape for two days. All she

did was sleep. It was a fast thing. She needed a third day to rest, but Emma was herself the day after that."

"This was a few weeks ago?"

"It was about two weeks before she died," Monica said.

"Did Emma enjoy the night out? Did she talk about it with you?" Shelly asked.

"I guess she enjoyed it, but she'd wanted Peggy and me to be there. She didn't say much to me about the get-together because she got so sick right after and was out of commission for a few days."

Shelly gave a nod. "Are you friends with Dawn Barry? I met her once at the leather shop in town."

Monica shook her head. "Dawn's a bit of a dip. She likes to drink, party. She's kind of loud and dramatic. She's not really someone I'd spend a lot of time with."

"Emma liked her?"

"Well, not really. She thought Dawn was immature. Dawn works at the pub at the resort in addition to the leather shop so she was around the resort all the time and ran into Emma quite a bit. Emma was nice to Dawn, but she didn't really consider her a friend."

"Dawn seemed very upset over Emma when I spoke with her at the leather shop," Shelly said.

"Well, that's what I mean," Monica said. "Dawn loves to attach herself to a situation that really doesn't involve her. She'd act like Emma was her best friend. She'd put on a show about her supposed grief. I think she loves the attention she gets from it. I don't mean to sound hard-hearted. I'm sure Dawn feels badly about Emma, but she's always very dramatic about everything. I think Dawn needs the attention. I think she craves it. Everything is about Dawn, about her feelings. Some people are like that."

"Have you seen Charlie since Emma died?" Shelly asked.

"I dropped some food off at their house. I talked to Charlie for a little while. He seemed like he was in a hurry to get away from me." Monica blew out a breath of disgust. "Good ole Charlie. He had the best wife anyone could ask for. Emma did everything in that marriage, paid the bills, managed the household, raised the kids, worked full time, took classes in her field to stay current, took a second job to pay off the debts *Charlie* accumulated." Monica looked pointedly at Shelly. "You know what I think? I think Charlie is happy to be free of his wife. When I talked to him the day I dropped off the food, he didn't seem all that upset about losing his partner."

Shelly thought back to the interview with Charlie she'd sat in on and recalled sensing the same thing about Charlie. "Do you think it's possible Charlie had something to do with Emma's death?"

Monica folded her hands and rested them on the tabletop. Shelly could see the woman's knuckles were white from gripping her hands so tightly together.

Monica said, "Charlie is a person I wouldn't be at all surprised to learn was Emma's killer. That guy can't be trusted."

15

S helly and Juliet rode their bikes to the resort to meet a group of hikers for a half-day hike on the mountain trails. The day was spectacular with the sun shining strong and the air cool, but not cold. The hike would take three-hours round trip and would pass fields, streams, and lakes and would take the group of fifteen hikers up rocky hills and ledges and along trails through the forest.

Shelly and Juliet only knew a handful of the people and introductions went around as everyone greeted one another before heading up the mountain.

Carrying a variety of snacks and a water bottle in her backpack, Shelly had also tucked a painkiller into her bag in case her leg started to bother her. She knew improvement was slow in coming and that the limp might be permanent, but she'd been pleased recently with the amount of physical activity she could manage before any pain and soreness started to kick in.

Talking with two vacationers to town, Shelly pointed out other trails the two women might want to try another day and gave them some history of the mountains and the towns that had sprung up in the area.

Juliet was up ahead walking with a woman who'd lived in Paxton Park for about fifteen years. Pamela worked as an emergency room nurse at the hospital and she was on duty the night Emma Pinkley was brought in.

After thirty minutes, the group arrived at a scenic overlook and they paused to sip water and take in the beautiful sight of the land below spreading out before them.

Juliet introduced Pamela to Shelly. "Pam was working the night Emma was brought in to the hospital."

"I was glad I'd never met the woman," Pamela told Shelly. "It's always a shock when someone you know from town comes into emergency with a serious issue. Being a resort town, we usually get athletic injuries ... broken bones, concussions, a cut or a gash that might require stitches, things like that. Of course, we also get the heart attacks, appendicitis attacks, trauma, dehydration, people with flu but, even in hunting season, we rarely ever get a gunshot wound."

Juliet gave Shelly a look. "We were talking about Charlie."

"Charlie wasn't working a shift that night, was he?" Shelly asked for clarification.

"No, he wasn't," Pamela said.

"We were talking about Charlie's *behavior*," Juliet told her friend.

"I've worked with Charlie for years. He's a good nurse, he knows his stuff...."

Shelly waited for the *but*.

"But, he can also be a pain. He thinks he's a gift to all women, or he acts like he is. It's good to have someone upbeat in emergency, someone who can joke or make you laugh. It can be a tough place to work. Charlie thinks he's funny, but his jokes are always off-color and he makes some of us uncomfortable. I always cringe when I see on the schedule we're working the same shift."

"Has anyone told Charlie his jokes are offensive?" Shelly asked.

"I haven't. You'd think he could figure it out by people's body language and facial expressions. When people don't laugh and they frown instead, you'd think he would get the message," Pamela said with a sigh. "Charlie doesn't get it, or if he does notice that we don't appreciate his humor, he just doesn't care and goes on with it anyway."

"Did he talk about Emma?" Shelly asked.

"Not much, and when he did, it was always some disparaging remark about his *old lady* and how she doesn't let him do his thing, she doesn't get him, she's too controlling." Pamela groaned. "I couldn't stand his immature ways. It could be like working with a twelve-year-old."

"Did you get a hint that his marriage was in trouble?" Shelly felt like the neighborhood gossip, but if she was going to help Jay find information that could lead to Emma's killer, then she had to swallow her pride and, sometimes her good manners, and ask the questions that needed to be asked.

"I don't know how his wife hadn't kicked him out long before now. I don't know how she could stand him," Pamela said. "But, I also don't get why she married him in the first place. Charlie's a strange one."

Thinking that *strange* was an odd way to describe the man, Shelly asked, "Does Charlie do his job well?"

"I have no complaints about how he does his job," Pamela said. "It's everything else. He has no filter."

The hike leader suggested they move on and everyone fell into line and headed for the trail that would lead further up the mountain. Shelly, Juliet, and Pamela hiked together into the woods at the back of the line.

"How do you mean he has no filter?" Juliet asked.

"He blurts out whatever comes into his head," Pamela said. "It's often something dirty or some comment about someone's looks or some talk about how hot some celebrity is. It gets old really fast. I'm not sure the man thinks about anything else. I don't know how he manages to control his mouth when he's treating a patient."

"Do you think Charlie might have violent tendencies?" Juliet questioned.

Pamela stopped on the trail and stared at Juliet with wide eyes. "You mean...?"

"Have you ever noticed Charlie losing his temper?" Juliet asked.

"I don't think so. I've seen him annoyed and

angry and agitated, but I haven't witnessed any physical aggression," Pamela told her. "Are you asking if I think Charlie had something to do with his wife's death?"

"Did Charlie ever talk or make comments about wanting out of his marriage?" Shelly asked.

"He implied sometimes that he wouldn't mind being free of his marital constraints," Pamela said slowly, thinking back on Charlie's chatter. "I took it to mean he wanted an 'open marriage' where he could be free to see other women." The woman's forehead wrinkled in thought. "That idea could be an incorrect interpretation though. Maybe Charlie *did* want to be free of his marriage." After a minute, Pamela asked, "Do you think Charlie might have killed his wife?"

"That's a question we don't know how to answer," Juliet said.

The group approached a steep, rocky section of the trail and the hikers concentrated on where they stepped as they made their way up and over the rocks and ledges. Even the best conditioned of the hikers were puffing and out-of-breath when they'd finished climbing the rocky terrain.

Pamela took a long drink from her water bottle and then with narrowed eyes, she asked Shelly and

Juliet, "Have you heard about Charlie's ... well ... his escapades?"

"His cheating?" Juliet asked.

"Exactly," Pamela said with a frown. "He was a notorious cheater. Sometimes, he even hit on women who came into the emergency room with a sick parent. Charlie would wait to flirt, of course, until the news on the parent was good. He, at least, had the sense not to ask someone out when her parent was in the middle of a health crisis."

Juliet shook her head. "The guy is sickening."

"Did Charlie hit on his colleagues in emergency?" Shelly asked.

"Not that I've ever witnessed, thank the heavens," Pamela said. "He saved that for every other department in the hospital."

"He must have a reputation. His antics must be well-known in the hospital?" Shelly asked.

"A lot of people are aware of Charlie. But, a lot of people aren't." Pamela shook her head. "And there is no shortage of willing participants."

Juliet let out a moan of distaste.

"Is Charlie involved with other women at the moment?" Shelly asked.

"When isn't he?"

"Women at the hospital?"

"I've seen him with someone who doesn't work at the hospital," Pamela said.

"Recently?"

"Oh yes. Charlie never rests. He's been with this woman off and on for a long time. Maybe a year? Although I haven't seen her around a lot for the last few months. She came to visit him sometimes when he was at work. Of course, Charlie flirts and puts the moves on other women while he sees this one."

"When was the last time you saw him with this woman?" Shelly questioned.

Pamela looked sideways at Shelly. "The afternoon before his wife got killed."

Juliet and Shelly shared expressions of disgust.

"They were busy together in the supply room." Pamela looked like she might spit. "I needed to get something from in there, but the door was locked. We have a smaller supply area closer to emergency, but what I needed was out so I went down the hall to the other supply storage room. I heard some sounds from inside. I heard Charlie's voice in there. I pounded on the door and then I took off."

Juliet couldn't help a little smile forming on her face. "You didn't wait around to see them come out of there?"

"I didn't. But Charlie hurried back into emergency and I saw his *friend* walk past the door on her way out."

"Gosh," Juliet said. "They have to see each other in Charlie's workplace? They can't wait until after his shift is over?"

"Guess not," Pamela said. "Like I said, lots of willing participants."

"Do you know the woman's name?" Shelly asked.

"I try not to pay attention."

"What does she look like?" Juliet asked.

"She's blond, short, slender, nice figure. I'd say she's in her early to mid-thirties. Blue eyes, wears a lot of makeup, false eyelashes."

Pamela's husband called to her from the front of the hiking line and gestured with his hand. "Pam, come see these birds over by the lake."

"I'll catch up with you in a bit." Pamela waved at her husband, started up to where he was standing, but stopped for a second and said, "You know, I think I heard Charlie call that woman 'Dawn'. I'm pretty sure, anyway." She turned and headed off to talk to her husband.

Juliet narrowed her eyes. "Dawn? Could it be Dawn Barry? The woman who works at the leather shop? The one who claimed to be Emma's friend?"

"Sounds like one and the same." Anxiety gripped Shelly's chest and held on tight.

16

"The records indicate that Steven Carlton's phone was in the vicinity of his home on the evening Emma was shot and killed," Jay said.

"But like you said before, his phone might have been at home, but Steve may not have been there," Juliet said.

Shelly carried in a tray of lasagna and set it on the trivets so the wood of the small dining table wouldn't get damaged. "If he planned to hurt Emma and he had his wits about him, he knew that the phone companies could pinpoint a phone's location. So Steve left on his little trip to follow Emma without his phone."

Serving Juliet and Jay, Shelly then placed a

square of lasagna on her plate and sat down to join her guests. Justice sat on a soft kitty bed in the corner of the room with her paw curled under, watching and listening to the people.

"There's one thing that bothers me about that though," Shelly said as she sprinkled some Romano cheese over her dinner. "If Steve left his phone at home and brought a gun along with him, it seems he had vengeance on his mind and planned from the start to hurt Emma. That would be premeditation."

"It sure would." Jay put some dressing on her salad.

"But why would he want to hurt her?" Shelly asked. "If Emma noticed Steve following her and she pulled over to chew him out, I can see Steve losing his temper and wanting to hurt her after their confrontation. But I don't see why he would go after Emma with a plan to kill her *before* they argued on the road."

"Steve may have kept his gun and ammunition in the trunk of his car on a regular basis," Jay pointed out. "Lots of people do that especially if they have kids. They don't want the weapon easily accessible in the house so they lock the gun in the trunk. If Steve became enraged after having words with Emma on the road, the gun was in the car. He might not have planned to murder Emma. The idea came to him after their fight and the weapon was right there in the trunk."

"That could be what happened," Shelly agreed. "Emma may not have been forceful with Steve while she was working at Windsor. When she stopped to confront him on the road, she may have had enough of Steve calling her and following her around and she may have blown her top at him. Her reaction may have shocked him."

Justice let out a long, low growl.

"If he didn't plan on killing Emma when he left his house," Juliet asked, "why didn't he take his phone with him? Why leave it at home?"

"The man could have forgotten it," Jay suggested. "Or maybe he wised-up about the phone giving away information on his whereabouts. He probably hoped to meet up with Emma and didn't want a phone company record of it."

Shelly thought of something. "Steve could have bought one of those no-contract, prepaid phones from a retail store to use. It would be hard to trace one of those back to him."

"I was just going to say that same thing," Jay told them. "Steve may have had more than one phone that he used in order to hide his activity from his wife, should she ever look through the bill to check the phone numbers he called. In fact, when I had him come into the station for another chat, I asked him about a second phone. He denied having more than one, but who knows?"

"How did the second interview with him go?" Juliet asked her sister.

"Much like the first one. Lots of denials, even when I caught him in a lie or an omission. He had an answer for everything. He said he only wanted to be friends with Emma." Jay rolled her eyes. "Right."

"Nobody can vouch for him being at home that evening?" Juliet asked.

"No one can verify that Steve was at home. He was sweating bullets during the interview," Jay said.

"Maybe he *is* guilty then," Juliet said.

"If I was being questioned by the police and I had no alibi for where I was when a crime took place," Shelly said, "I'd be sweating bullets, too. Not because I was guilty, but because the police *thought* I was guilty. Perspiring can't be equated with being guilty. The guy is a harasser and a creep, but that doesn't mean he killed Emma."

"That's right," Jay said. "If Emma had lived and Steve Carlton kept up his harassment of her, Emma could have gone to court for a restraining order on the guy."

"He seems guilty to me," Juliet muttered.

"I also talked with Charlie Pinkley again," Jay told them.

"What did he have to say?" Shelly asked.

"I spoke with him about his affairs. I asked if he was presently seeing Dawn Barry. He denied it. Charlie told me that he'd had a fling with Dawn in the past, but it was long over."

"'Long over' must mean something different to Charlie than it does to the rest of the world," Shelly said. "The nurse who worked with Charlie claims to have seen him with Dawn on the day Emma died."

"But did the nurse actually see them together?" Jay asked. "She said Charlie came back to the emergency department and she saw Dawn walking down the hallway to exit the hospital. It sounds like the nurse didn't see them together."

"Surely, the timing of Charlie's return to the emergency room and Dawn leaving the place can't be coincidental," Juliet said. "They must have been together."

"Try telling that to a judge," Jay said. "Dawn could say she was at the hospital for any number of reasons. Even if someone saw them together, it doesn't mean anything. They could simply say they ran into each other. Anyway, having an affair doesn't mean Charlie killed his wife."

"But what if you put a few things together?" Juliet asked. "Not long ago, Emma took out a life insurance policy, Dwayne overheard Charlie at the hospital say he wanted out of his marriage, Charlie is a serial cheater."

Shelly added, "Plus, Charlie drove an hour to the mall to buy boots he could have purchased in town for the same price and he couldn't find his phone right before he left the house so he went to the mall without it. That was convenient, wasn't it? No cell tower pings to see where he actually was."

"But none of that would stand up in court," Jay said. "None of those things can incriminate the man. Add all of those things up ... they don't prove murder."

Shelly let out a groan. "I know you're right, but those things sure make me want to keep Charlie on the suspect list."

"I second that," Juliet said. "Charlie is definitely a suspect."

Jay nodded her head. "This thing is a puzzle with a thousand pieces."

THE WOMEN SAT in Shelly's living room talking about anything but the case using the time to relax and enjoy one another's company. Justice joined in by sitting on the sofa between Shelly and Jay and requesting scratching behind her ears which they were happy to oblige.

With a yawn, Jay said, "Time for me to head to bed before I fall asleep on this comfortable couch."

Justice stood up and growled low in her throat.

"What's wrong, little one?" Shelly asked. "You don't want Jay to leave?"

Juliet stretched and yawned. "Let's see if I can stay awake long enough to drive you home. Will you come with me, Shelly, and keep me awake on the ride back?"

"Sure." Shelly chuckled and went to get her jacket. "It's only a ten-minute drive, but if I don't go and you fall asleep, I'll never hear the end of it," she teased her friend.

Jay's house was only about eight miles away. She lived there with her husband, Eddie. They'd been married for over twenty years and had an eighteen-year-old son, Mike, who was away at college in Boston.

"You've got the house to yourself for a couple of days," Juliet said. "You should have a few wild parties while Eddie is away. Jay's husband, a financial advisor, was in Boston to attend some meetings and visit with their son.

"I didn't think about doing that," Jay kidded. "I don't know if I have time to pull a wild party together on such short notice."

Juliet pulled the car into the long driveway and stopped in front of the garage. Jay thanked her sister for the ride and Shelly for the delicious dinner, and as she was opening the passenger side door, Shelly glanced to the house. "Jay. Hold up. Is your front window broken?"

With her hands on her hips, Jay stared at the front of the house while Shelly and Juliet got out of the car and went over to stand beside her.

"Maybe you should call the police," Juliet suggested.

"I am the police." Jay strode towards the front door, opened it, and entered with her sister and Shelly right behind her. When she flicked on the light, the two women behind her gasped.

The living room was in a shambles, with furniture overturned, books knocked off the bookcases, and the windows at the side of the room smashed. A good-sized rock sat on the rug. It had been thrown through the front window.

Jay let out a string of curses and stormed into the kitchen to see if there was any damage there. The room was untouched, but Jay stood at the kitchen table, trembling.

Shelly and Juliet walked up behind her and looked over the woman's shoulders.

In the center of the table, was a smashed photograph of Jay, her husband, and their son.

A knife had been stabbed into the middle of the photo.

Juliet put her arm around her sister as Jay whipped her phone from her jacket pocket and placed a call. Her voice rattled with rage. "It's Jay. I need some officers and a team at my house. Now."

17

It was hours before Shelly, Juliet, and Jay headed back to Juliet's place. Juliet had to work hard to convince her sister to come back home to sleep at her house.

"The windows are broken," Juliet had said, "you certainly can't stay here until they've been fixed."

Jay had fussed for quite a while about needing to stay at home, but finally she relented and packed a small overnight bag.

Officers and a detective combed through the house and around the outside looking for any clues or evidence. A police photographer took pictures of everything and doors, knobs, and furniture were dusted for fingerprints despite the law enforcement officers believing nothing viable would be found.

"I'd bet money the perp wore gloves," one of the investigators said, "and we won't be finding any fingerprints."

Jay had been shaken by the photo of her family having a large knife stuck into the center of it. Worry, fear, and fury had mixed together in equal parts until rage became the overriding emotion. "Some creep broke into our home, touched our things, is trying to intimidate me. It won't work." She called her husband and son to report what had happened and Eddie wanted to drive back from Boston right away, but Jay pooh-poohed the idea.

Two officers found some sheets of plywood in the basement and with Juliet's and Shelly's help were able to board up the three broken windows. When Jay saw the windows had been closed up, she went on and on about staying in the house, but Juliet wasn't having it and practically dragged her sister to the car. "I'll drive you to work in the morning like we planned. You can use one of the squad cars during the day, until your usual vehicle is out of the shop." Jay's car was in for service and would be ready in the afternoon.

While waiting for Jay to be done at the scene, Shelly wandered around the house trying to use her powerful intuition to understand who might have done the damage.

"I'm not picking up on anything," Shelly admitted to Juliet.

Shaking her head, Juliet told her, "You're not a psychic. You take things that happen during the day and your mind works on them during a dream. That's how you make connections and figure things out. You can't walk through the house expecting to 'feel' or 'sense' the vandal."

"Oh, I know," Shelly admitted. "I wish I could help with the whole mess. I don't like to see Jay upset."

Juliet had moved a little closer to her friend. "Do you think this break-in has something to do with Emma Pinkley?"

"I've been thinking about that," Shelly said. "Jay has very recently talked to both Steve Carlton and Charlie Pinkley. Maybe one of them is afraid Jay's investigation is getting too close, that she'll figure everything out soon."

"So the person breaks into her house and tries to frighten Jay off?" Juliet grunted. "They sure don't know my sister. This violation of her home is only going to make her double-down, work more hours, leave no stone unturned. I pity the person who did this. Breaking into a police officer's home? This guy is in big trouble."

"But which guy did it?" Shelly asked. "It's doubtful there were any witnesses. I bet whoever did it, left their phone at home so they couldn't get pinged by the cell towers and I also bet there won't be any fingerprints left behind either." Looking around the room, she said, "Whoever did this is full of fury and resentment. Jay needs to be careful."

SHELLY COULD BARELY KEEP her eyes open when they returned from Jay's house and pulled into Juliet's driveway. After mumbling goodnights to each other, Shelly climbed the steps to her front door and went inside to see Justice waiting for her. The cat moved around her owner's legs, rubbing and purring. Shelly picked up the Calico and hugged her. "It's been a long night, Justice. I can't wait to get into my bed."

As soon as Shelly's head hit the pillow, she fell into a deep sleep ... and then the dream came again.

Back in the same restaurant, the women sat around the table talking and laughing. Dawn Barry was there sitting next to Emma.

Lauren eyed her sister and then looked over at Emma.

The money rained down from the ceiling again, and then it formed the cyclone, shot up high, and disappeared.

The women were having drinks. When Shelly reached for her wine glass, Lauren took it away, swallowed all the wine, and then turned the glass upside down.

Shelly tried to ask why she'd done that, but no words would come out of her mouth. She moved her hand to touch the wine glass, but Lauren shook her head slowly back and forth.

Shelly looked over at Emma to see the woman's face turning pale and pasty. Her eyelids slipped halfway closed and her hand shook when she held her glass. She almost seemed to be swaying slightly as if she was battling to keep herself awake.

Dawn smiled and spoke to Emma, but Shelly wasn't able to hear what she'd said to her. Suddenly, a loud crash made everyone jump and startled sounds escaped their throats. A picture on the restaurant wall had fallen with a smash to the floor.

Shelly stood near the ruined painting and her heart began to race when she saw it was a picture of Emma, prone on her back, her glass in her hand, a cut on her wrist bleeding from being sliced by a broken shard.

After her eyes popped open and she realized where she was, Shelly ran her hand over the cat's soft fur. "What does it mean, Justice? What's this crazy dream trying to tell me?" She rested back on the pillow and after thirty minutes, fell back to sleep.

Having only a few hours of rest didn't keep Shelly from waking with the sun. She texted Juliet to invite her and Jay over for a quick breakfast before heading to work and when the two women arrived, Shelly put out heaping platters of pancakes, eggs, and home fries.

"How are you doing?" Shelly asked Jay.

"Much better after seeing this hearty breakfast." Jay poured herself a cup of coffee.

"Did you get any sleep?" Shelly put her napkin on her lap.

"Not much," Jay admitted.

"Neither did I," Juliet chimed in and rubbed her eyes. "It's going to be a long day on the mountain with just a few hours of sleep. I couldn't turn my brain off. I'd close my eyes and then see all the broken windows and the trashed room in Jay's house."

"Same with me." Jay said. "I couldn't stop

thinking about who was responsible for the break-in. My mind wouldn't rest and I became infuriated all over again."

"What about you?" Juliet glanced over to her friend. "Where you able to get some sleep?"

Shelly set her mug down on the table and said softly, "I had the dream again."

"Lauren was there?" Jay asked.

Shelly nodded.

"Did the same things happen in this one that's happened in the other dreams?" Jay questioned.

"Yes, but this time when the painting fell, I saw Emma was the subject of the portrait. She was unconscious in the painting. Emma was on the floor, on her back. She looked dead." Shelly's heart raced. "What's this dream trying to tell me?"

"The smashed portrait could be symbolic of Jay's broken windows," Juliet offered. "Emma's in the painting because the vandalism has something to do with Emma's murder."

Shelly took in a deep breath and wished the dreams and the discussions of the nighttime images didn't bother her so much. "Emma looked awful, like she was sick or exhausted or about to pass out. Her face was as white as snow. She couldn't keep her eyes open. I know she looked terrible to symbolize the onset of her illness after getting home from the restaurant. But, I don't know. I feel like I'm supposed to be seeing something else … that the dream is trying to get me to understand something." Shelly lifted her hands in a helpless gesture. "But what is it? What am I missing?"

"Do you recognize the people sitting around the table?" Jay asked.

"Only Emma and Dawn Barry. I don't know what the other women look like who were there that evening with Emma." Shelly picked up her fork and then set it back down again. "I'm there, and Lauren is, too, but it feels strange, like we're only watching the people around the table, we're really not part of the group. The other women don't seem to notice that we're there with them."

"In other dreams you've had, do you interact with the other people in the dream?" Jay asked.

Shelly thought for a moment. "Well, in regular dreams sometimes I do, but in the Lauren dreams, I'm often just watching and I don't speak very often. Lauren never uses words, either."

"What things have been in all of the recent Lauren dreams?" Jay asked.

"Let's see, the money swirling around, the women sitting around the table, and the wine glass,"

Shelly said. "The smashed painting showed up in two dreams and this is the first time I was sure Emma was at the table."

"What does Lauren do when the money starts swirling around?" Jay questioned.

"Not much. We both glance at it, but it doesn't seem to bother us."

"And the wine glass?" Jay asked. "In every dream, Lauren takes the glass away from you and turns it upside down?"

"Yes. She drinks the wine before she turns it over."

"Does she seem upset, or frightened, or angry?" Juliet asked.

"None of those things." Shelly shook her head. "Lauren seems matter-of-fact, maybe a little annoyed or maybe, determined, once she seemed sad. She does not want me to drink that wine."

Justice let out a howl making the three of them jump, and then all of sudden, Jay, Shelly, and Juliet sat up straight, each one thinking the same thought.

"The wine," Juliet said. "Your sister doesn't want you to drink it."

"There's something wrong with the wine," Jay suggested.

A light went off in Shelly's head. "Only me and

Emma. We're the only ones who have wine glasses. Emma drank from hers."

Jay stood up. "I need to talk to the other women who were at that gathering. I need to find out if any of the others got sick after being at that dinner."

18

In the middle of the afternoon, Shelly and Juliet left their jobs at the resort to head for Jay's house to clean up the rest of the break-in mess and to meet with the contractor who was coming to work on the windows.

The contractor's truck was at the end of the driveway near the garage and two men were at the front of the house measuring the picture window. Juliet spoke with them about what needed to be done and the men assured her the window work would be completed by early evening. The owner of the company knew Jay's reputation as an honest, hard-working member of law enforcement and a valued member of the community. The owner was sending a second crew to the house in order to get the job done that day.

Juliet and Shelly entered the house and stopped at the threshold, the mess of the room making their hearts drop from the assault on Jay and her family.

"It looks worse in the light of day." Juliet's throat was tight with sadness and anger.

Shelly touched her friend's shoulder and squeezed. "We'll have it spotless by the time Jay gets home. She's not alone. She's got the whole town behind her, looking out for her."

The two friends replaced every book on the bookshelves, used a small shovel to remove the larger pieces of broken glass from the floor, ran the vacuum over the floor and the rugs to suck up small shards of glass, straightened the furniture, dusted and washed down the coffee table and side tables to rid the surface of any tiny pieces of the broken windows, and then went into the kitchen.

The framed, broken photograph of Jay, Eddie, and their son still rested on the tabletop. The knife had been removed and taken to the police station leaving the mangled photo behind.

Juliet got a folder from Jay's desk and slipped the sliced up picture inside of it. "I'll put the photo aside in case the detective wants to take another look at it. I know where Jay had this picture done. The photographer has a shop in town. Let's go there later and see if she can produce another one. I'll have it framed for Jay and Eddie."

Shelly agreed it would be a thoughtful thing to do. "I'm sure they'll appreciate it."

When Juliet went outside to answer a question for the contractors, Shelly washed off the kitchen table and returned to the living room to get the dust cloths they'd left in there. One had fallen to the floor and when she bent to pick it up, Shelly noticed something sticking out from under the baseboard.

Walking over to the wall and bending down, she picked up a phone just as Juliet came into the house.

"What's that?" Juliet asked.

Shelly held it out. "It was partially under the baseboard. It must have gotten kicked under there last night when the officers were in the room looking for clues."

Juliet took the phone from her friend. "It's not Jay's. Maybe it fell out of one of the officer's pockets. I'll turn it on and see if there's an emergency contact or family contact information."

When the phone came on and Juliet opened the

contact information, she gasped and pushed the phone at Shelly. "Look at it."

Glancing at the list of contact information on the screen, Shelly's heart dropped. *Emma, Aubrey, Mason, the hospital.* She made eye contact with Juliet. "It's Charlie Pinkley's phone."

Juliet sank onto the sofa and when she spoke, her voice shook. "He was in here? He did this damage? Charlie Pinkley?"

"We shouldn't have touched it. Our fingerprints are on it now." Shelly went into the kitchen, took a plastic sandwich bag from the drawer, and slipped the phone into it. When she returned to the living room, a stunned Juliet was still sitting on the sofa.

"Come on. Let's take this to the police station," Shelly suggested. "Jay needs to see it."

JAY'S FACE hardened like stone when she saw the phone and the contact list and once she collected herself, she called for an officer to take the phone away and enter it into evidence collection where it would be tested for fingerprints.

"Charlie Pinkley." Jay said the man's name like it left a bad taste in her mouth. She sat in her chair behind the desk and took a deep breath. "The man claimed that his phone was lost. He had to get a new one." Jay looked at the two women sitting across from her. "Thoughts?"

"A couple of thoughts," Shelly started. "One, Charlie was in your house. He did the damage. He killed Emma. He may feel trapped and frightened by your investigation and is trying to intimidate you."

"What's your second thought?" Jay asked.

"Charlie was in your house. He did *not* kill Emma, but he feels like you're going to pin the murder on him and he'll end up going to prison. He isn't known for good judgment. He is known for impulsive behavior. He wanted to strike out at you so when he saw the house was empty, he broke in, and dropped his phone."

"Those are my thoughts as well," Jay nodded. "I think there's a third thing, too. What if Charlie found his old phone? He'd already bought a new one. He decided to give the old phone to someone else. That particular someone broke into my house and the phone slipped out of his or her pocket ... or, how about this ... the person dropped it intentionally to point law enforcement to Charlie."

"You mean to make Charlie appear to be the guilty one?" Juliet asked.

"Possibly," Jay said.

"Too many possibilities," Juliet moaned. "When we came here, I assumed Charlie was the guilty one. Now it's possible someone who had his phone broke into your house and either lost the phone in there or dropped it specifically to finger Charlie."

"Who could that someone be?" Shelly asked.

"I hate to say it," Jay began, "but maybe Charlie gave the phone to one of his kids. Perhaps, one of them has a king-sized grudge against his or her parents."

"Oh," Juliet almost gasped. "One of the kids? One of the kids might have murdered Emma? It's too terrible to even consider."

"Charlie might have given the phone to a friend," Jay said. "A few times when we've upgraded our phones, we've given the old one to a family member or a friend. It's not uncommon to do that. Charlie may have given his phone to someone besides the kids."

"This is an impossible puzzle." Juliet rubbed at her forehead.

"What will you do next?" Shelly asked.

Jay sighed, "First, the case detective and I will have another talk with Charlie. Then we'll see where we go from there."

On the sidewalk outside of the police station, Shelly and Juliet complained about how complicated the case was and spoke admiringly about Jay's investigative skills.

"I wish this thing was over," Juliet muttered. "I'm worried for Jay's safety. It makes me feel helpless."

Shelly suggested, "You wanted to go visit the photographer who took the photo that was damaged during the break-in. Why don't we head over to the shop and ask whether she still has the photos from the family shoot she did with Jay? You can order it and pick out a frame. It will take the worry off your mind for a while and it will be a nice thing to do for Jay's family."

"Good idea. Let's do it," Juliet agreed and they turned around to head to the other end of Main Street.

Two photographers owned the shop in Paxton Park doing photo shoots, portrait sessions, photo repair, and framing. Juliet spoke with Elise, the photographer who remembered doing the family shoot with Jay, her husband, and son. The woman went to the computer to look up the session's photos.

While she was searching, the second photographer came out of the back room alongside a woman carrying a little baby boy. The woman was medium height and slender, with green eyes and long, straight strawberry-blond hair.

Elise glanced up from the computer screen. "How did he do, Peggy?"

"He did great," the woman said.

The photographer said, "His photos are going to come out terrific."

While the woman held her baby and stood at the counter to pay and make arrangements to see the digital proofs, Shelly and Juliet smiled and cooed at the little boy.

The receptionist processed the payment. "Here's you receipt, Mrs. Lane," the young woman said.

Shelly looked at the woman. *Peggy? Peggy Lane? Emma's good friend?* "Are you a friend of Monica Jones?"

A look of surprise washed over Peggy Lane's face. "Yes, I am," she said cautiously.

"I work in the kitchen at the resort's diner," Shelly said. "I've talked to Monica several times when she comes in for breakfast. She mentioned your name. I'm sorry for the loss of your friend, Emma."

Peggy relaxed and rubbed her baby's back.

"Thank you." She asked Shelly some friendly questions and shared a few words with her about Emma.

"Monica mentioned that you and she missed the dinner out with Emma not long ago," Shelly said.

Something passed fleetingly over Peggy's face. "I did go to the dinner. My little one wasn't feeling well that night, but when my husband got home, I decided to go meet them at the restaurant. Dinner was almost over by the time I got there, but I had a soft drink with them."

Shelly said, "Monica told me Emma got really sick right after the get-together."

"She did, yeah. She was sick for two full days."

"Did anyone else in the group come down with the flu or whatever it was?"

"I don't think Emma had the flu," Peggy said.

"What do you think caused her illness?" Goosebumps started to form over Shelly's arms.

Peggy seemed like she was going to say something, but then changed her mind. "I don't really know. Maybe her drink didn't agree with her."

Emma's drink? The dream of Lauren taking her drink away from her flashed in Shelly's brain and a shiver ran over her skin.

Just as Shelly was going to ask the woman about

the drink, Peggy said, "I need to get my boy home for a nap. Nice to meet you."

Peggy and her son left the shop, but the feeling of unease that Shelly experienced when the woman mentioned Emma's drink remained ... and caused Shelly's heart to race.

19

"Why would Peggy Lane say Emma's drink might not have agreed with her?" Shelly asked. "Why not say maybe her *meal* didn't agree with her? Isn't that more likely?"

"Maybe Emma had too much to drink and Peggy didn't like her friend overdoing it." Juliet lifted a spoonful of ice cream from her bowl.

"But my dream," Shelly said. "In my dream, Lauren takes the wine glass away from me. She doesn't want me to drink it."

"But Lauren doesn't take the wine glass away from Emma," Juliet said.

"It's symbolism," Shelly said. "I'm representing Emma."

"Really?" Juliet scrunched up her forehead. "These are very complicated dreams."

Shelly plopped onto the sofa with a second bowl of ice cream and mumbled, "Lauren should take the ice cream bowl away from me."

"What does the floating money in the dream represent?" Juliet asked as she dipped her finger in the ice cream and offered it to Justice to lick. The cat didn't hesitate.

"I don't know. I haven't figured that out."

"I don't understand why all this symbolism shows up in your dreams. Why not just come right out with it instead of being so mysterious and confusing?"

"Lauren doesn't speak in the dreams," Shelly explained. "So I have to figure things out."

"Well, couldn't she write things down for you? Write you a message so you don't have to connect the dots. So you don't have to figure out what every little thing means. What if it's so confusing you can't figure it out and you get it all wrong?"

Shelly shrugged. "Then I guess I get it wrong."

Juliet sniffed. "It's not a very efficient way to work."

"It's the way it is though." Shelly put the bowl with her half-eaten ice cream on the side table. "I'm feeling antsy. I need some fresh air. Want to go for a walk?"

Justice quietly jumped up onto the side table and worked on the remaining ice cream. Shelly noticed and took it away from the Calico. "No, Justice. Too much of that will make you sick."

Standing up to take her bowl to the kitchen, Juliet said to the cat, "You don't want the vet to think Shelly poisoned you."

Suddenly, Juliet stopped walking. She and Shelly shared a look.

"Poison?" Juliet asked with wide eyes.

"The wine glass. Is that why Lauren doesn't want me to drink it?" Shelly shuddered. "Was there poison in Emma's drink? Did someone try to poison her? Is that why Emma got so sick that night? Did Peggy Lane notice something?"

Juliet asked, "Is that why Peggy said maybe Emma's drink didn't agree with her?"

Shelly picked up her phone and did a search for Peggy Lane's address. "The Lanes live right off Main Street." She looked up. "Should we go over there and ask her what she meant about Emma's drink?"

"I don't know. She might think we're odd. We only talked to her for a few minutes. I don't think she'd confide in us. I'm going to call Jay and tell her what we think." Juliet placed the call and spoke with her sister while Shelly went to get their jackets.

"Jay said she'll arrange a meeting with Peggy. That makes me feel better. It's best that the police handle all of this."

The young women walked along the brick sidewalks to the town common. Tourists and townspeople wandered around the common looking at the Halloween scarecrows set up for the contest. The nightly bonfire blazed at the far end of the common and a crowd gathered around to warm up from the chilly October evening.

Store windows were lit up, pumpkins and chrysanthemums decorated every establishment, and the golden glow of the streetlamps made the cozy town seem warm and snug nestled beside the majestic mountain range.

Julie sighed. "Why can't everything always be pretty and nice and pleasant?"

"Because of greed and jealousy and power and hate," Shelly told her.

Rolling her eyes, Juliet said, "I guess that sums it up."

"Which one of those is the reason Emma Pinkley got killed?"

"Probably all of them." Shelly shoved her hands in her pockets.

Juliet let out a groan and they walked the length of Main Street before turning around and heading back the other way, occasionally stopping to look into some of the shop windows.

Juliet paused in front of a window display of winter jackets and noticed someone waving at her from inside the store. It was Linden Parker, from Windsor Manufacturing, the young woman who came into the conference room a few days ago to speak to Jay and Shelly about Steve Carlton and his behavior towards Emma.

Linden came out of the store. "I came into town with my boyfriend. We had dinner and now he's shopping for a new ski parka."

The three women chatted for a few minutes.

Linden asked, "Did you hear about Steve Carlton?"

"What about him?" Juliet asked.

"He got fired. For harassing some of the other employees."

"He did?" Shelly's jaw had dropped.

"Yup," Linden said. "And guess what else? Steve's wife is leaving him. She found out about his obsessions with other women and is divorcing him. I bet she knew about Steve and his weird ways a long time ago, but she's finally had enough. We heard Steve was acting oddly at home, cleaning his guns at the kitchen table and muttering. His wife got scared, told him he should go see the doctor for anxiety and depression. Steve yelled and swore at her and that was the last straw. She left him."

"Wow." Juliet was amazed at the turn of events.

"Steve owns weapons?" Shelly asked as a zing of nervousness raced through her stomach.

"That's what we heard. A rifle and a handgun. Their house is on the market, too. Steve's wife has taken the kids and has gone to live with relatives."

"Is Steve living in the house?" Shelly asked.

"A guy at work told us Steve is living there until it sells. I heard he's a mess with his life falling down all around him."

"I almost feel sorry for the guy," Juliet said. "Almost."

A good-looking man appeared at the shop door and held up a ski jacket for Linden to see.

"I'm going back inside to help my boyfriend pick something out," Linden said. "Nice to see you again."

When she closed the door behind her, Shelly and Juliet stared at each other.

"I wasn't expecting that," Juliet said with a shake of her head.

"You can say that again." Shelly blew out a long breath. "It sounds like Steve Carlton is going off the deep end."

Juliet's eyes widened. "What if it was Steve who broke into Jay's house and trashed the living room?"

"The mess of it and the way the knife was stabbed into the picture suggested rage and violence, like someone was out of control. The way Linden described Steve makes him sound like he's out of control, angry, and depressed."

"We need to tell Jay," Juliet said.

"What about Charlie's phone?" Shelly asked. "It was in Jay's house. If Steve is the one who broke in, how do we explain Charlie's phone being in there?"

Juliet thought for a few moments. "Jay wondered if Charlie gave his old phone to someone. Maybe Charlie knows one of the construction guys who were there to repair the windows. Stranger coincidences have happened."

"Have they?" Shelly asked skeptically.

A woman's voice could be heard loudly cursing and the two friends turned towards the sound to see Dawn Barry standing near a parked car outside of the leather shop. Dawn cursed again and kicked the driver's side door with her foot.

"It looks like someone else is out of control," Shelly said. "Let's go see what's up."

Crossing to the other side of the street, Shelly and Juliet approached Dawn Barry.

"Are you okay?" Juliet asked. "Do you need some help?"

"My stupid car won't start. I called a garage to come tow it away," Dawn fussed. "I have to wait for them to get here. Stupid car is always breaking down."

"Can we get you a coffee or tea while you wait?" Shelly asked.

Dawn took a deep breath and sighed. "No, thanks anyway. I'm exhausted. I've been working all day since the shop opened."

Knowing that Dawn had been seeing Charlie Pinkley while claiming to be Emma's friend didn't make Shelly feel too sorry for the harried woman. She decided to ask Dawn a few questions.

"Have you seen Emma's family recently? You told us the other day you were a close friend of hers. I was wondering how her husband and kids were doing," Shelly said trying to get Dawn to talk.

"I haven't seen them." Dawn looked down at the ground.

"Are you friends with Charlie?" Shelly asked.

Dawn's head snapped up, her eyes flashing. "What's that supposed to mean?"

"Were you friends with Emma *and* Charlie?"

"No. Charlie's a loser. Everyone knows that."

Juliet took a quick look at Shelly.

"Why do you say that?" Shelly asked, wanting Dawn to say more. "Why is he a loser?"

"Because he is. He's an idiot. I can't stand him." Dawn practically growled.

Juliet asked, "Was Charlie mean to Emma?"

"Yes. He was a jerk to her. I don't know how Emma could stand him." Dawn poked her toe against the curb.

Shelly said, "I was talking to one of Emma's friends. The friend told me Emma got really sick not long ago. A group was out for dinner with her and when Emma got home, she was terribly ill. The friend told me she came down with something similar the next day. The friend said she wondered if they'd had food poisoning. Did you go to that dinner?"

Dawn looked at Shelly with narrowed eyes. "I was there that night. Who told you she got sick?"

"Monica Jones," Shelly said.

"Monica got sick, too?"

"She told me she did. Did you all eat something different?"

"I thought so."

"So you didn't get sick?" Shelly asked.

"No, I didn't."

"If it was food poisoning, I'll make sure I avoid that place," Shelly said. "Did Emma and Monica order the same thing?"

"I don't remember."

"What about the drinks?" Shelly asked.

"What about them?" Dawn asked.

"Did Emma and Monica drink the same thing? I wonder if there was something wrong with the wine?"

"I have no idea." Dawn seemed agitated and checked her phone for the time. "Where is that tow truck?"

"Can we drop you at home once the tow truck comes?" Juliet asked.

"What?" Dawn snapped. "Oh. No, thanks. I'm good."

Shelly was pretty sure Dawn was *not* good.

20

Carrying a watering can to the front porch, Shelly gave her pots of flowers a drink. Justice acted as supervisor sniffing each pot after it had been watered and when she'd checked them all, the Calico sat on the step next to Shelly.

"Are the pots satisfactory?" Shelly asked the cat.

Justice rubbed her cheek against Shelly's arm and purred.

The afternoon was pleasantly warm and the young woman and the cat soaked up the sun together while sitting on the front steps. Shelly would have liked to have gone for a bike ride on the mountain trails, but Jay was coming by in a few minutes to talk with her about the case.

Jay's husband had returned from Boston and hired a company to install a security alarm for the house. They should have done it long ago, he said, especially with Jay in law enforcement since the job could attract revenge seekers and people who didn't particularly care for officers of the law.

Looking up at the mountains rising over the town, Shelly could see some of the ski trails weaving in and out of the forest. There wasn't any snow yet, but it wouldn't be long before the snowboarders and skiers descended on the mountain and filled the hotels, inns, and bed and breakfasts. Paxton Park attracted tourists all year round, but the winter season was the most crowded and Shelly looked forward to the hustle and bustle of people enjoying the area.

The sound of a car's engine caused Shelly and Justice to turn their heads to see Jay's police cruiser pulling into the driveway. Jay climbed out and joined the woman and cat on the porch.

"The sun's great today," Jay lifted her face to the rays. "It feels good."

Justice stepped onto the police officer's lap and settled down, purring.

"This cat doesn't miss a chance, does she?" Jay

chuckled and ran her hand over the multi-colored fur.

"Are the new windows in?" Shelly asked.

"They're all set and looking good. They needed upgrading anyway," Jay said.

"Are you feeling okay about what happened?"

"I'm only surprised it hasn't happened sooner. Sure, I was boiling mad when we walked in and saw the mess. It's a violation, someone entering your home, trying to intimidate you, frighten you. It can make a person feel down about humanity." Jay gave a shrug. "But the feeling doesn't last long. I need to focus on the fact that the majority of people are good-hearted."

"Sometimes that isn't easy, is it?" Shelly asked.

"We have our moments, but like I said, the pessimism dissipates. I can't do this job if I'm not optimistic and hopeful."

"Are you feeling that way right now?"

"I am." Jay smiled.

"Good," Shelly said. "Because I need to tell you what we heard last night about Steve Carlton."

"I heard some information through the grapevine," Jay said. "It seems things are falling apart for Steve."

"That's right." Shelly proceeded to tell Jay what

she'd learned from Linden Parker. "It sounds like he's falling into depression. And the part about the guns was worrisome."

"I agree. As a precaution, we sent an officer over to the Carlton's house to do a wellness check on Steve. The names of some doctors and counselors were left with him. The officer offered to make an appointment for Steve, but the man declined," Jay said. "He can't be forced to seek medical care."

"No, I suppose not," Shelly said. "Not yet anyway. I hope he doesn't do anything stupid with those guns." With her thoughts turning to Emma, she added, "He may already have done something stupid with them." After a few moments thinking about Steve Carlton, Shelly told Jay, "We ran into Dawn Barry last night."

With a raised eyebrow, Jay said, "You and Juliet were busy last night."

"Dawn was cursing and kicked her car. It had broken down. It seemed an overreaction, but I guess, from what I've heard about her, her behavior can be like that."

"Did she talk to you?"

"She did. I pretended not to know about her 'fling' with Charlie. I asked her if, in addition to being friends with Emma, she was a friend of Charlie."

"And what did she say to that?" Jay asked.

"She told us Charlie was a loser, an idiot, that he wasn't good to Emma, that she couldn't stand him."

"Trouble in paradise?" Jay asked.

"It certainly seemed so. Dawn was angry. It didn't seem like she was pretending to dislike Charlie, it seemed like she really couldn't stand him."

"Maybe they had a falling out," Jay said. "Maybe the 'fling' is over."

"What was the reason for that, I wonder," Shelly said.

"Maybe now that Emma is gone and Charlie is free of his wife, he wants to play the field."

Shelly shook her head. "That guy. Whoever gets mixed up with him is in for a bad time."

"Speaking of Charlie," Jay said with a serious tone, "I have some news about his phone."

Shelly adjusted her position on the step to better face Jay. "What is it?"

"Through the phone records, we've just learned that Charlie's phone pinged a cell tower in the vicinity of Paxton Park on the evening Emma was murdered."

With an open mouth, Shelly stared at Jay.

"The phone hadn't pinged any towers again until the day you found the phone in my house and turned it on," Jay said. "The report also indicated that a text from Charlie's phone was sent to Emma around the time she dropped Leena Tate at the automotive garage to pick up her car. About an hour after the text was sent, a second text was made from Charlie's phone to Emma's."

"No one replied to the text?" Shelly asked.

Jay shook her head.

"What does it all mean?"

Justice lifted her head and growled low.

Jay said, "It means that Charlie's phone was in or close to Paxton Park on the night that Emma died. The texts were made to Emma's phone, then Charlie's phone went quiet for days until you found it and turned it on in my house the night of the break-in."

"So Charlie lied about going to the mall." Shelly thought out loud. "But he had his receipt for the boots. Did someone else go there and buy the boots for him so he would have a receipt?"

"That could be," Jay said. "Charlie's daughter claims he went to the mall so unless she's lying, he left the house that night to go somewhere. And if he didn't go to the mall, who might have gone in his place while he was busy finding Emma?"

Shelly's eyes widened. "Dawn Barry?"

"That is my thought."

"What do you think happened? Emma's murder was all over the news. Did Dawn suspect Charlie was the killer? Did she get scared because she went to the mall for him? Maybe she worried he would say she was in on the murder and knew all about it. He could say she was his accomplice."

"It's an interesting scenario, isn't it?" Jay asked.

"Wow." Shelly thought of something else. "Were fingerprints found on the knife that was stuck into the photograph at your house?"

"Nothing."

"Then the person who broke in wore gloves or wiped down the knife. What about Charlie's phone? Were there fingerprints on it?" Shelly asked.

"Only yours and Juliet's." Jay's face looked tired.

"Charlie's phone was wiped and cleaned, too," Shelly said. "So that makes me think Charlie didn't give his old phone away to anyone who lost it in your house. If he had given it away and it got dropped in the house, there would be fingerprints on it." Shelly sat straight. "So whoever dropped the phone in your house may have intended to do so."

"Maybe you should join our police force," Jay gave the young woman a little smile.

Shelly speculated, "Another scenario could be that Charlie asked Dawn Barry to go to the mall, buy the boots, and keep the receipt for him. Charlie told Dawn he killed Emma, or she heard about it on the news or the radio. Dawn gave him the boots. For some reason, they ended their relationship. Who knows why? Then Charlie broke into your house and dropped his phone."

"Possibly." Jay nodded. "Now I need to find some real evidence."

Shelly's face clouded.

"What is it?" Jay asked.

"But, what about my dream? Lauren takes the glass away from me and turns it upside down. How does that relate to what happened to Emma?"

"Maybe it doesn't?" Jay said gently. "Maybe it's just a dream?"

Shelly looked out across her small front lawn to the road. "No, it isn't just a dream. Lauren is trying to tell me not to drink the wine. There was something wrong with the wine in Emma's glass the night she went to dinner with friends. It has something to do with her murder. I'm sure of it."

Justice let out a low hiss. The fur on her back stood up straight.

Shelly looked at the cat. "Justice agrees with me. Have you talked to Emma's friend, Peggy Lane, yet?"

"Only once, the day after Emma died," Jay said.

"Talk to her again. When Juliet and I spoke with her at the photography store, I was sure she was going to tell me something important. Go see her. Ask her about Emma's drink."

"It can't hurt," Jay said. "I'll arrange a meeting."

"I know I've been reluctant to believe that my dreams can reflect something important, something I miss about a situation when I'm awake." With a serious expression, Shelly looked at Jay. "I understand that most dreams are only dreams. But this dream of Emma at the restaurant is trying to tell me something. We can't ignore it. I'm sure of that."

21

J ack and Shelly held hands as they walked around the town common together. The night was surprisingly warm, but no one was complaining. Several musicians had set up on the bandstand and a good-sized crowd had gathered to listen. Food stands were selling cotton candy, candy apples, caramel corn, sausage sandwiches, and pizza slices. The bonfire blazed off to one side and lots of people stood close to watch the flames shoot high into the air.

Jack bought some cotton candy and he and Shelly sat on a bench to watch the people and nibble on the sweet, pink confection.

"I haven't had this since I was little." Shelly

smiled as she put a wad of the pillow-y candy into her mouth where it melted against her tongue.

"Neither have I. It's great, isn't it? Why has it taken me so many years to get some?" Jack pulled a long section of pink fluff off the white tube stick.

When they finished, Shelly and Jack wandered over to the bonfire and bumped into Patti, one of the adventure guides, and her sister, Loni. Jack introduced Shelly.

The four young people chatted for a few minutes and then Patti said, "I still can't believe what happened to Emma Pinkley. I knew her from working at the resort. She was such a nice person. Now, I look at people when we're in crowds and I wonder if one of them is the killer. It's a terrible feeling to think he could be walking around town and passing us on the sidewalk."

"Emma was always so cheerful," Loni said. "I can't imagine getting shot and driving back to town. It's a horrible thought."

"Do you work at the resort?" Shelly asked Loni.

"No. I work at a bank in Linville. I've been a teller there for years."

Shelly said, "Emma's mother lived in Linville. Is that how you knew Emma?"

"Not through her mother, no. Emma did some banking where I work," Loni said.

"At the bank in Linville?" Shelly tilted her head.

"Yeah. She had an account there." Loni cringed. "I saw her about an hour before she got killed."

"You did? She came into the bank?"

Loni nodded. "It was just before 7:30pm. We close at 7:30. Emma made a deposit."

"Why would Emma bank in Linville?" Shelly asked knowing Emma was the only one who could accurately answer that question. "There's a branch of the same bank right here in town."

Loni smiled, "Well, you know. When it comes to finances, sometimes people want a little privacy."

"Do you think that was what Emma wanted?" Shelly asked. "Was she after privacy?"

"If I had to guess, I'd say that was the reason she used our branch."

"But, why?"

Loni shrugged. "We don't ask that question when people open accounts."

"Was Emma's husband on the account?" Shelly asked.

Loni bit her lower lip. "I'm not supposed to give out any information like that. But I'm not working in the bank at this moment so let's just say there wasn't any reason for his name to be on the account."

"Why not?" Shelly didn't understand.

Loni said, "The account was actually in Emma's sister's name, Evelyn Billings Wentworth. But, it was clear that it was Emma's money that was in the account."

"Why would she put her money in an account with only her sister's name on it?"

"Think about it," Loni said. "Why would you put your money into a secret account under someone else's name?"

"Because you don't want someone to know about it," Jack said.

"Exactly," Loni told him.

"I don't get it," Shelly said. "Are you sure it was Emma's money? Was she trying to help her sister by providing her with money?"

"My bet would be Emma was putting money aside because she didn't want her cheating rat of a husband to find out about it," Loni said. "I shouldn't be telling you this stuff, but Emma is dead so what does it matter if I talk about it? Emma made a huge deposit an hour before she was killed. All in cash. I won't tell you how much she put in her account, but it was a lot of money."

"Now the money will go to Charlie?" Jack asked.

"No. In fact, it will go to her sister, Evelyn. Anyone can make a deposit to someone else's account. Some banks don't allow cash deposits to a different account, but our bank does. Only the owner of the account can actually withdraw the money."

"You think Emma was hiding money from Charlie by putting it into an account under her sister's name?" Shelly asked.

"That's my theory. That way, Charlie couldn't gamble it away."

"When Emma came into the bank, did she seem nervous or worried or upset about anything?"

"No." Loni shook her head. "She seemed like herself. The transaction only takes a few minutes though. She could have been hiding concerns that she had. I probably wouldn't have picked up on it."

They moved from discussing Emma to other topics of conversation and after about fifteen minutes of chat, Shelly said, "We're going to head off now. Nice to meet you."

She took Jack's arm and they moved away from the bonfire.

"Why did you want to leave?" Jack asked.

"I'd like to go see Emma's sister, Evelyn. Care to go for a little drive?" Shelly asked her boyfriend.

"Now?"

"It's not late. I don't think she'd mind."

"Okay then. Let's go," Jack said.

"I HOPE we're not bothering you," Shelly said to the woman who answered the door. "I was here days ago with Jayne Landers-Smyth from the Paxton Park Police Department. Do you have a few minutes to talk?"

Emma's sister, Evelyn, stood staring at the couple on her front porch. She blinked several times and then nodded and invited them inside. "I remember you. Come in."

Taking seats in the living room, Jack sat quietly next to Shelly on the sofa.

Evelyn asked, "Is there some news?"

"Oh, no. I'm sorry. I'm not here on official business," Shelly said. "There was something I wanted to ask you about. I've heard recently that Emma was at the bank here in Linville about an hour before she died."

Evelyn's lower lip trembled. "Yes, she was. She

made a deposit. She came here right afterwards to give me the deposit slip."

"The account is in your name only?"

Evelyn clutched her hands together. "Emma wanted me to set up an account that she could deposit to. All the money belonged to Emma, but the account was in my name."

"Why did your sister want a secret account?" Shelly asked.

Evelyn rubbed her forehead. "She didn't trust Charlie anymore. She knew he cheated and had affairs. She'd known it for years. He has the gambling problem. Emma felt like he didn't contribute to the family as he should have. She also thought she and Charlie would end the marriage sooner than later. She was coming to the end of her rope with him."

"Emma was hiding the money from Charlie?"

Evelyn said, "Emma was sure he would gamble it away and then when they divorced, she'd have nothing. She'd been saving for years. She'd put any extra cash aside and when she managed to save a good amount she'd go to the bank in Linville. Emma wanted the account in my name so that Charlie couldn't get at it."

"What will happen to the money now?" Shelly asked.

Evelyn said, "Emma was adamant that Charlie never get his hands on the money. I'm going to pretend it's mine and when the kids, Aubrey and Mason, are older, I'll give them the money."

"I have something else to ask you," Shelly said. "There's something that's been bothering me. When Emma went out to dinner with her friends, she was very sick when she got home. Did Emma talk to you about her illness?"

Evelyn's face looked hard. "She thought she came down with the flu. I didn't think it was the flu. I think Charlie slipped her something before she left the house."

"What do you mean?"

"I've always thought Charlie did something to try to get rid of Emma. I wondered if he'd poisoned her."

Shelly's eyes went wide. "Poison?"

"How could Emma get so sick so quickly? No one else caught her illness. Not the kids, not Charlie, not me or our mother."

"It's possible that no one would catch what Emma had," Shelly suggested. "On occasion, only one family member comes down with an illness."

"Emma didn't have a cold or the flu or a virus or whatever," Evelyn's eyes flashed. "Someone tried to poison my sister. I know it. I just have no way to prove it."

"You didn't bring this up with the police?" Shelly asked.

A miserable look washed over the woman's face. "No. What's the point? They'd just think I was crazy. It's too late to prove anything. Maybe a blood test at the time would have shown something in Emma's system, but it's too late now."

"Did you discuss the possibility of poisoning with Emma?"

"I did. At first, Emma thought I was letting my imagination get away from me, but then she wondered if I might be on to something."

"Do you think Charlie murdered Emma?"

Evelyn looked down at the floor. "Yes, I do."

"Does Charlie own a gun?" Shelly asked softly.

When Evelyn lifted her face, tears glistened on her cheeks. "He killed my sister. He has to have a gun."

22

"I've been concerned with how it might look to have a private citizen sitting in on interviews that I do," Jay told Shelly when the young woman arrived at the police station late in the afternoon.

"Oh. I'll leave then," Shelly said. "We don't want to do anything that might compromise the investigation."

"Hold on," Jay said lifting a piece of paper from her desk. "I'm hiring you for contracted services to consult on a case by case basis. That way everything is aboveboard."

Shelly was dumbfounded. "But I don't have any credentials."

"I've discussed it with the higher-ups. I told them

how you've helped out on the past two cases and it's been approved. So if you agree to get paid for the time you consult with me, you need to sign here." Jay pointed at the line on the bottom of the page and handed Shelly a pen.

"I should probably read it first," Shelly kidded.

Jay nodded. "You won't get rich on the hourly payment, but at least I don't have to feel guilty about taking up some of your time. This way, everything is documented."

After reading over the one-page contract, Shelly signed at the bottom. "I'm not sure how I'm going to juggle three part-time jobs."

"You'll manage." Jay shook the young woman's hand. "Welcome to the Paxton Park Police Department. Now let's go interview subject number one."

Shelly settled on a stool behind the one-way glass and watched as Charlie Pinkley was brought in for questioning.

"I'm going to get right to it, Mr. Pinkley," Jay said. "We've received new cell phone record reports that have been updated with information regarding your phone." She let the words hang in the air.

"Meaning what?" Charlie asked with forced bravado.

"On the evening of your wife's death, cell towers tell us your phone location was in Paxton Park."

Charlie's shoulders relaxed. "I told you I couldn't find my phone. I lost it sometime that afternoon so, of course, it would be here in town."

"It was picked up by a tower on the other side of town," Jay said. "Near Linville."

"It must be an error." The man's facial muscles tightened. "It couldn't have been near Linville." Charlie's eyes took on a look of alarm. "I wasn't in Linville, if that's what you're suggesting. I was at the mall, an hour away from here. I showed you that receipt."

"You could have asked someone to pick up the boots at the mall for you. That someone would have given you the receipt."

"What? Why don't you go to the mall. Go to that store. They'll tell you I was there."

Jay let out a long breath. "Two of our officers paid that store a visit. They don't remember the person who bought those boots."

Charlie's hand came down hard on the table. "You're trying to railroad me. You're making this up. I was in that store. They must have security tapes or something. Ask for those. Look at the tape."

"The store's security video camera is broken."

His cheeks reddened, Charlie began to sputter, but then his face went stony and he sat without saying a word.

"Do you own a gun, Mr. Pinkley?" Jay asked.

"What? No. I don't like guns."

"Do you have a gun in your possession?" Jay asked.

"Absolutely not. Ask my kids, if you don't believe me."

"On the night Emma met a group of friends for dinner, she returned home extremely ill," Jay said. "Did she take anything before leaving the house?"

"Like what?"

Shelly wanted to yell through the two-way glass. *Did you poison Emma?*

"Medication of any kind?"

"Not that I know of." The man shrugged.

"Did she have something to drink?" Jay asked.

"You mean booze?"

"I mean anything at all."

"I don't know." Charlie's tone revealed his exasperation. "Maybe she had a cup of coffee."

"Was Emma allergic to anything?"

"No. No allergies." Charlie crossed his arms over his chest in a defensive posture. "Why are you asking me this stuff?"

"I am trying to determine if something besides a virus might have caused Emma's distress."

Charlie gave a tight chuckle. "What do you mean, like poison?"

Jay stared at the man.

"You're serious? Come on. Really? Look I have to be somewhere." Charlie stood up. "I'm free to go, right?"

"Yes, you are," Jay told him.

For now, Shelly thought as she watched Charlie Pinkley storm out of the conference room.

FORTY-FIVE MINUTES LATER, Shelly was behind the two-way glass again, this time watching Jay interview Dawn Barry.

The woman's hair looked dry and over-bleached. Her eyes were lined with black liner and she had on false eyelashes. Dark circles showed under her eyes. Dawn looked thinner and her face seemed drawn.

Shelly wondered if Dawn drank too much or took some drugs. Her appearance didn't seem to match her chronological age.

"Thanks for coming in, Ms. Barry," Jay said with a welcoming smile. "I just have a few questions for you." Jay gave her spiel about how it was difficult to ask and answer personal questions and she apologized in advance about having to ask some of those types of questions.

Dawn gave Jay a withering look. "Planning to ask about my love life?"

"In a manner of speaking," Jay said. "We understand you were involved with Charlie Pinkley."

Dawn's face turned red. "Has that loser been telling tales?"

"We'd like to hear things from you, Ms. Barry. Did you date Charlie?"

"Yeah, I did. Everyone makes mistakes, don't they?" Dawn sneered.

"How long did you date?"

"I don't know. Maybe six months. Things were on and off with Charlie."

"When was this?"

"Oh, let's see." Dawn picked at her fingernail. "I got tired of him about six months ago."

"And that's when your relationship ended?" Jay asked.

"There wasn't a *relationship*. We had some fun together." Dawn raised one shoulder.

"You were friends with Emma Pinkley?"

Dabbing at her eyes, Dawn said, "Yeah. I can't

believe she's dead."

Shelly didn't quite believe Dawn's sudden display of grief.

"How would you describe your relationship with Emma?"

"Good friends," Dawn said.

"You were good friends with Emma, but you were seeing her husband?"

Dawn frowned. "Lines got crossed that shouldn't have been crossed. I'm sorry about going out with Charlie."

"What made you stop seeing him?"

"Like I said, I got tired of him."

An angry expression crossed Shelly's face. *You got tired of him? You didn't stop seeing him because you felt guilty about dating your friend's husband?*

"Did you start seeing Charlie again over the past month?" Jay asked.

Dawn's eyes narrowed. "Did he tell you that?"

"No, he didn't. I'm asking you."

"And I'm telling you, no I didn't."

"Did Charlie own a gun?" Jay questioned.

"I don't know." Dawn leaned back in her chair. "He talked about getting a gun. He thought it would be good protection. I don't know if he got one or not."

"Do you own a gun?"

"No. Too dangerous."

"On the night Emma went out for dinner with you and some other women, she was very sick when she arrived home," Jay said. "Did she seem like she was coming down with something during the meal?"

"Emma seemed a little tired. She didn't complain about anything. I heard she got pretty sick."

"Did you ask her about it?"

"No, I didn't want to bother her."

"Did you come down with something similar?"

"I got a headache the next day and I felt a little sick to my stomach."

"Did Emma drink a lot that night?" Jay asked.

"I wouldn't say so."

"Did Emma have allergies to anything?"

"I don't know about that. She never told me anything about allergies."

"Can you tell me what you were doing on the day and evening that Emma was killed?" Jay asked. "Can you run through your day for me?"

"Why?" Dawn looked defensive.

"We ask this of everyone." Jay nodded to encourage the woman.

"Um, okay, I guess. Let's see. I worked at the leather shop in town until about 3pm. I stopped at the store for a few groceries and then I went home and did laundry and took a nap."

"What store did you shop at?"

Dawn told her. "I wasn't in the store long. I just got some bread and milk and some other stuff."

"Did you go anywhere else that afternoon?"

Like to the hospital to see Charlie? Shelly thought.

"No, I don't think so."

"Did you happen to run into Charlie that day?"

"Charlie? I don't think so. I don't remember seeing him anywhere."

"Did you go by the hospital that day?" Jay asked keeping her voice even.

"The hospital? No, why would I?"

"To visit someone? For an appointment, maybe?"

"No."

Sitting on the stool behind the two-way glass, Shelly's eyebrows went up in disbelief at Dawn's memory problems.

"And what about in the evening?" Jay questioned.

Dawn tapped her index finger against her chin. "In the evening? I don't know if I went out. Oh, yes, I did. I decided to drive over to that nice store *Something Special*. Do you know it? It has really nice clothes, but they're very expensive."

Something Special was about four miles from the center of Paxton Park.

"Did you buy something there?"

"No." Dawn shook her head sadly. "There was a great dress in the window that I liked. I drove by the store earlier in the week and noticed it. I parked in the lot, but before I got out of the car, I started to feel guilty about spending a lot of money. I sat there for a few minutes and then I changed my mind. I went home."

"So you didn't go in?"

"No. I would have liked that dress, but I decided to do something sensible instead and not blow my money on something I really didn't need."

"Where were you when you found out Emma had been killed?"

"I was at home watching television. A news alert came across the bottom of the screen about a woman who had been shot here in town. I didn't know it was Emma until I went to work the next day and someone told me." Dawn put her hand over her heart. "I almost had a heart attack."

Shelly stared through the glass at the woman. Something about Dawn sent pricks of unease darting across her skin.

23

L ight was streaming into the bedroom when Shelly woke with a start. Her sleep shirt stuck to her back, wet with perspiration, and her heart raced. On the bed curled next to her owner, Justice jumped to her feet when the young woman bolted up into sitting position.

"It's okay, Justice. I had that dream. Again." Shelly had the same dream three times during the night, and each time it caused her to wake in fear.

The dream was the same. Lauren was in the restaurant with Shelly and the other women gathered around the table. The cash fell from ceiling, like it always did, and then the bills fluttered around, shot back up, and disappeared.

Lauren took her sister's glass away from her,

drank the wine, and overturned the glass onto the table. The same as always.

But the last dream of the night had an added twist.

Lauren glanced across the table at someone and when Shelly followed her eyes, she could see that her sister was looking at Emma. Emma was listening to Dawn Barry tell her something Shelly couldn't hear. Both women had glasses of red wine.

Making eye contact with Shelly, Lauren slowly shook her head and then looked back to Dawn and Emma.

Shelly watched as Dawn held Emma's glass in her hand and moved the glass so that the wine swirled around. The two women were looking across the table to a dark-haired woman who was telling them a funny story. Emma's attention was pinned on the brunette.

Someone hurried over to the table. It was Emma's friend, Peggy Lane, who had decided to join the group even though she knew it was late and they'd be finishing up their meals. Everyone greeted Peggy and when Dawn looked away, Peggy glared at the back of the woman's head before pulling a chair over and squishing in between Emma and Dawn.

The look Peggy gave Dawn had chilled Shelly

and emotions raced through her body with such force that her eyes popped open and she shot up to sitting position.

"What was that all about?" Shelly patted the cat trying to calm herself.

After eating breakfast and showering, Shelly decided to walk to the bank in the center of town to get some cash before heading to the diner to bake the day's breads and sweets.

Heading onto Main Street, a woman pushing a stroller waved to Shelly and crossed the street to greet her.

"Morning," Peggy Lane said. With a smile, she nodded to her little son in the stroller. "We were up very early this morning. We're on our way to my parents' house for a visit."

The women chatted about their day, the baby, Halloween, and the upcoming town festival.

"How are you holding up?" Shelly inquired about how Peggy was handling the death of her close friend.

"It helps to have the baby. He keeps me busy and keeps my mind from dwelling on the nightmare of Emma's murder."

Shelly asked, "Do you know much about Dawn Barry?"

Peggy's face changed. "I know enough about her."

"She was friendly with Emma?"

"Emma really didn't like her," Peggy said.

"Was that because of Charlie?" Shelly asked pointedly.

With a look of surprise, Peggy glanced at the young woman walking by her side and let out a sigh. "That had a lot to do with it, yes." Gripping the stroller's push-bar, she added, "Imagine someone pretending to be your friend when that someone is having an affair with your husband?"

"I don't even know what to say about that," Shelly shook her head. "It's so terrible. Do you think the affair was on-going?"

"Emma thought Charlie and Dawn were seeing each other again," Peggy said. "I don't think the marriage was going to last too much longer."

"Emma mentioned divorce to you?"

"She did. She talked about preparing to leave Charlie. I think she came to the conclusion that he would never change and there was nothing more she could do to try and make it work. She was tired of the cheating and the gambling and having a messy life. Emma had decided that she and the kids would be better off if the marriage was dissolved."

"Had she told Charlie yet?"

"Not yet," Peggy said. "She wanted to talk to an attorney first."

Her early morning dream flashed through Shelly's mind. "When I met you in the photography shop, I asked about Emma getting so sick after the dinner out with friends. You said something like maybe Emma's drink didn't agree with her. What did you mean? Did she drink a lot that night?"

"Emma never drank a lot. She was always careful and never over did it," Peggy said.

"Do you think there was something wrong with the drink?"

Peggy didn't answer right away, but then she said, "I don't like Dawn. I don't trust her. I think she's rotten to the core and has no values. She lacks concern for anyone except herself. It's always all about Dawn and what she wants, what she needs. She can't see beyond the end of her own nose."

"What about Emma's drink though?" Shelly persisted.

"When I was walking over to the table to join them that night, I thought I saw Dawn pick up Emma's drink."

An icy cold sensation gripped Shelly's stomach.

"Dawn made an odd motion with her hand. I

don't know. I suppose I have an overactive imagination," Peggy said. "It seemed like Dawn slipped something into Emma's wine."

"You think Dawn tampered with Emma's drink?" Shelly had to carefully control her voice volume to keep herself from shouting.

"Oh, probably not. It's a ridiculous idea." Peggy moved her hand around in the air. "I pulled up a chair and plopped myself at the table right in between Emma and Dawn."

Just like in my dream this morning.

"Then Emma got sick," Shelly said. "Maybe there *was* something in her glass. Should you mention this to the police?"

"Oh, gosh, no. I don't want to embarrass myself. It was my dislike of Dawn that fueled my paranoia. The police would just think I was some hormonal new mom whose imagination had run away with her, that I was jumping to foolish conclusions."

The women walked along the sidewalk for a few more minutes.

"Is that what you really think?" Shelly asked. "That you jumped to conclusions about something in Emma's wine?"

Peggy stopped to adjust the blanket around her baby and then she looked at Shelly. "I don't know. I don't know what to think. It doesn't matter what happened that night. Emma is dead. My friend is gone." Brushing at her eyes, she said, "I turn off here. My mom lives down this street. I'll see you later."

Shelly continued along the sidewalk to the bank thinking that Peggy might not be right about one thing.

What happened that night probably *does* matter.

WHEN SHELLY ARRIVED at the diner, she went right to work baking pies and muffins and several pumpkin breads. The diner was busier than usual and Melody and the waitstaff were straight out while Henry manned the grill cooking like a madman.

"Why is it so busy today?" Shelly asked, jumping in to help the older man prepare the meals.

"There's another dang conference booked at the resort this week." Henry added some burgers to the grill. "We need to expand this kitchen and hire another cook on a part-time basis to help out when the resort is fully-booked."

When the lunch crowd finally slowed, Henry swigged a bottle of ice cold water and mopped his brow with a towel. "We did it ... and without a single customer complaint."

With a smile, Shelly teased the man. "It must all be due to my helping you out."

"I'm going to hire you as second cook." Henry kidded as he cleaned down the grill. "Forget about baking." He gave Shelly a wink. "Thanks for your help."

"Anytime. I'll send you my bill." Shelly returned to her baking and spent the next two hours making three different kinds of pies. When she'd finished cleaning up, Henry turned to her with a slightly panicked look.

"Melody went home. There are two platters of food in the walk-in cooler for the Pinkleys. A friend of theirs ordered from us for delivery to the house to arrive late this afternoon. I forgot about the delivery. I hate to ask, but could you take my van and bring the food over to the Pinkley house?"

Shelly's face went pale and her heart banged like a hammer against her chest wall. She hadn't driven a car since before the accident that took her sister's life. "I...."

"If you can't do it, I'll call Melody to come back. She has a doctor's appointment right now. She can come back here once she's finished." Henry looked up at the clock.

One of the wait staff peeked into the back room. "A group of ten people just came in. I wanted to warn you."

Henry groaned.

"I'll drive the food over to the house." Shelly's voice shook as she said the words. "I'm glad to do it."

She *wasn't* glad to do it, but she wanted to help Henry and it was only about four miles to the Pinkley place.

Henry thanked her over and over again as he took the large platters from the fridge and ran outside to put them in his van. He handed Shelly the keys. "I can't thank you enough."

"I'll be back in a little bit." Shelly got into the driver's seat and immediately broke out in a cold sweat. "If I don't pass out first," she mumbled and pressed the button to start the engine. The vibration of the vehicle caused Shelly to have to rest her head on the steering wheel and she began to talk to herself. "I am ... able to do this. I am .... safe. I am ... going to drive this van." Over and over she repeated the phrases, and then she sat up and put the van into drive. Her inner core felt like it was full of ice.

All the way along the country lanes, Shelly

muttered positive phrases and affirmations and when she finally pulled to a stop in front of the Pinkley home, she felt like her muscles had turned to jelly. Placing both hands on her cheeks, she said, "I did it. I did it. I made it here."

The school bus pulled to a stop to let Aubrey Pinkley off at her home as Shelly was removing the first platter from the rear of the van.

"Oh, hi. It's you." Aubrey came over to see what Shelly was doing. "I stayed late at school and had to take the late bus home."

Shelly explained that she worked at the diner and was delivering some food for them ordered by a friend.

"I thought you worked for the police," Aubrey said.

"I do. I have three jobs actually."

Aubrey slung her schoolbag onto her back so she could carry one of the platters for Shelly. They chatted as they walked up the front walkway to the porch.

"That's Dawn Barry's car in the driveway next to my dad's car," Aubrey observed.

A sinking feeling pulled at Shelly's heart as she recognized the vehicle Dawn drove.

Stepping up to the front door, Aubrey opened it

and went inside, holding the door for Shelly to enter.

As soon as they were in the small foyer, a shot rang out.

Aubrey let out a piercing scream. "Dad!"

Aubrey dropped the platter she was holding and was about to dart towards the kitchen when Shelly grabbed the girl's arm, dropped her own platter, and yanked the front door open, shoving Aubrey outside.

Hearing running feet heading their way, Shelly was about to dart outside after Aubrey when a voice said, "Hold it right there. I've got a gun."

Shelly slammed the door so the person wouldn't see Aubrey standing on the front porch and then turned the dead bolt so the teenager wouldn't try to get back inside.

And with her heart in her throat, Shelly slowly turned around.

24

Dawn Barry stood a few yards from Shelly with a gun in her hand. The gun was pointed at Shelly.

"You." Dawn growled. "Where were you a few minutes ago when Charlie pulled this gun on me?"

"Charlie threatened you?" Shelly asked in a tiny voice. She could feel the lies that slipped from Dawn's mouth bumping against her skin.

"He was going to kill me." Dawn still held the gun on the young woman.

"Where is he?"

"In the kitchen. He said he was going to kill me. We fought."

"You got the gun away from him?" Shelly went along with Dawn's story to buy some time.

"The gun went off when we were fighting."

Unconsciously, Shelly stepped a little to the right to move away from the muzzle of the weapon.

"Don't move," Dawn said.

"Why are you holding the gun on me? Why don't you put it down?" Shelly used a gentle tone of voice.

Dawn stared at Shelly.

"Is Charlie...?"

"I don't know."

"Did you call for an ambulance?" Shelly asked.

"No."

"Why don't we call for help," Shelly suggested.

"No."

Trying to think of something to say that would help her to get away from Dawn, Shelly looked down at the boxes of food on the floor. "I brought food from the resort diner. I dropped them when I came in. I'll get something to clean up the mess."

"I told you not to move." Dawn's expression was of a cornered, wild animal. The whites of her eyes were huge. Some spittle showed at the corner of her mouth.

"We should go see about Charlie," Shelly tried to convince the woman. "Maybe we can help him."

"Charlie got what he deserved."

"What do you mean?" Shelly could feel cold

sweat dribbling down her back. She hoped Aubrey had called the police and that a squad car would arrive soon. *Hurry.*

"Charlie is a loser and a liar." Dawn's skin was pale, but her cheeks were blazing red. "He killed Emma, you know."

"Did he? Did he tell you that?"

"Yeah. He was so sick of her. He was so tired of her running his life."

"Was he mean to you?" Shelly wanted Dawn to think she was on her side.

"Not at first. He was real nice to me ... at first." Dawn's eyes hardened. "Then he dumped me."

"What happened?"

Dawn looked Shelly in the eye. "Charlie is a user. He uses people. He doesn't care about anyone but himself. He had to die. The world doesn't need people like him."

"Is Charlie dead?" Shelly asked with a tremble in her voice.

"I hope so." Dawn's hand shook a little and her eyes seemed to glaze over. "I loved him at first. He didn't love me. I figured that out. I thought the only reason he wouldn't stay with me was because of Emma ... and those kids."

A chill ran over Shelly's skin.

"If Emma was dead, then Charlie would be with me. That's what I thought but, it didn't work like that."

"You hoped Charlie would come back to you if Emma was dead?"

"He didn't. I took his phone from him. He didn't know I did it."

"Why did you take it?" Shelly asked. *Where are the police?*

"So I could trick Emma. So I could get her to come and help me."

"Help you with what?"

"I pretended to be Charlie. I pretended his car broke down. I used Charlie's phone to text Emma to ask her to come pick him up." A smirk twisted Dawn's lips into a sneer. "Only Charlie wasn't there on the side of the road. I was."

Shelly's heart pounded hard against her chest. "What happened?" she whispered.

"I shot Emma. It was me. I killed her. But, I'll tell everyone Charlie did it."

"When did you steal his phone?"

Dawn's face was pinched and tight as she looked at the floor of the entryway. "I went to talk to Charlie at the hospital. I tried to convince him to leave Emma. He wouldn't do it. I took his phone." A triumphant look crossed Dawn's face. "He didn't even know I took it."

"Why did you take it?"

"To use it against him. For dumping me. He's such a loser." Dawn's chest rose and fell … her breath coming fast and shallow. "Loser's don't dump me," she muttered.

Shelly took a step backwards. "I need to get back to the diner. Henry will be wondering what happened to me."

Dawn's head snapped up and she looked at Shelly with glazed eyes. "No. You have to stay here."

Some scuffling sounds could be heard in the kitchen and Dawn wheeled around. Just as Shelly turned for the front door, a young woman's scream rang through the air.

"Dad! Dad!"

Aubrey had entered the house through the back door to find her father on the floor.

Dawn hurtled down the hallway to the kitchen and Shelly chased after the woman.

Shelly screamed, "Aubrey! Run!"

Charlie was on his back on the kitchen floor with blood seeping through his shirt. His skin was deathly pale.

Aubrey, her long brown hair falling forward over

her face, knelt beside her father, holding his hand and wailing.

As she rushed into the kitchen, Dawn's hand came up and she pointed the gun at Aubrey, but before she could pull the trigger, Shelly barreled into the woman, knocking her off balance.

Dawn fell to the floor. The weapon dropped from her hand and skidded across the room.

Shelly scrambled to her feet, crossed the room, and grabbed the gun. Wheeling around, she pointed it at Dawn and yelled, "Sit on the floor. Put your hands behind your head. Don't you move."

Kneeling next to Charlie and keeping an eye on Dawn, Shelly used one hand to feel for a pulse on the man's neck and found a faint beating against her fingers.

"He's alive. Can you do chest compressions" she asked Aubrey.

Tears streamed down the teenager's cheeks and she stared blankly at Shelly.

"Stand up." Shelly yanked the girl to her feet and, without thinking, pushed the gun into her hand. "Hold this while I help your dad. Keep your eye on her." Kneeling again, she began to do chest compressions. "Did you call for help? Did you call the police when you were outside? Aubrey?"

Shelly turned her head to look up, and she leapt to her feet. *Oh, no.* "Aubrey," she said softly.

The teenager held the gun in two shaking hands and pointed it at Dawn's head.

Dawn had slumped over with her arms wrapped around her head, rocking back and forth on the floor, her body shuddering.

"She killed my mother." Aubrey's voice trembled as her finger moved to touch the trigger. "She shot my father."

With her stomach in a cold knot, Shelly moved her feet slowly across the floor. *No, no, no. Don't let this happen.* Fighting to keep her voice calm and even, she said, "Aubrey. Don't do it. Hand me the gun. If you shoot her, you'll be just as bad as Dawn. Hand it to me. You know it's the wrong thing to do."

Shelly slowly reached her arm out, her hand open. "Your mother loved you. She would never want you to do this."

Aubrey buckled at the waist, sobbing, and with a rush of relief, Shelly removed the gun from the teenager's hand and then wrapped the young woman tightly in her arms.

25

The police arrived soon after Aubrey had let go of the gun. The officers removed Dawn Barry from the house shortly after Jay and an ambulance arrived to the Pinkley home. Jay was surprised to see Shelly in the kitchen with her arm around Aubrey's shoulders. It took some time for the two of them to explain to the police what had happened.

Charlie survived his gunshot wound and was expected to make a full recovery. He was innocent, at least of his wife's murder. The man was a gambler and a philanderer and Shelly doubted he would ever be able to change his ways despite Charlie's new-found determination to do so. Shelly hoped he would prove her wrong.

Emma's sister, Evelyn, and her husband had moved into Charlie's house temporarily to help Aubrey and her brother and so they would not be alone while Charlie was in the hospital recovering. Evelyn had even suggested to Charlie that they sell their houses and buy a two-family home together in order to support and comfort the children. Evelyn was still working on forgiving Charlie for the way he disgraced his marriage, but that was going to take a very long time. Aubrey and her brother were the priority now.

Dawn Barry stole Charlie's phone on the afternoon before she killed Emma. She'd gone to the hospital to try and talk Charlie into getting back together.

The thought of killing Emma had been swirling around in Dawn's head for two months and she believed if Emma was dead, then Charlie would start seeing her again. At the hospital that day, Charlie told Dawn that it would not work out between them and that she should move on.

Enraged, Dawn took the man's phone and decided once and for all to murder Emma.

Dawn had tried previously to get rid of Emma on the night of the gathering in the restaurant. She'd secretly slipped a poisonous powder into Emma's wine which was the cause of Emma's violent two-day illness. Dawn was incensed that Emma survived. She was sure she'd put enough poison in the glass to kill her victim.

On the afternoon that Charlie rejected her once again, Dawn decided to put an end to Emma Pinkley. She wanted to be with Charlie. She also knew about the couple's life insurance policies and dreamt of a life with Charlie, free from monetary worries.

On the evening of the murder, Dawn, pretending to be Charlie, used his phone to text Emma twice. The first time to ask where Emma was, and the second time, to report that Charlie's car had broken down and to ask if she would come and pick him up.

When Emma arrived, Charlie wasn't there ... but Dawn was ... and when Emma's car rolled up beside Dawn, the woman pulled a gun on Emma and shot her in the chest while she was sitting in the driver's seat of her vehicle.

Dawn was hopeful that with Emma out of the way, Charlie would once again fall into her arms, but instead, he rejected her one more time. In a fury, Dawn broke into and trashed Jay's house. Charlie had rejected her advances for the last time and Dawn was ready to set him up for the murder of his wife. Deliberately leaving Charlie's stolen phone in Jay's house, Dawn set the plan in motion.

The truth was discovered, however, and Dawn Barry would be charged with first-degree murder for planning and executing the killing of Emma Pinkley.

As for Charlie's shopping trip on the evening Emma was killed, it turned out that the man had indeed gone to the Stockville mall to buy the boots, but he had another reason to drive all that way. Charlie was seeing a new woman in the town and he dropped by her house for a little visit.

It was the evening before Halloween and Juliet and Shelly had invited friends to Shelly's for a buffet dinner and then a walk into town for the annual Halloween Carnival.

Jack-o-lanterns, cornstalks, and mums decorated the front porch, and the scarecrow man with the pumpkin head they'd made three weeks ago sat in one of the rocking chairs on the porch. Justice was still wary of the thing and gave it wide berth whenever she had to walk past it.

The living room and dining room of Shelly's little rented house had been decorated with small wooden black cats, glass pumpkins, twinkling orange lights on the fireplace mantle, vases of orange and yellow flowers, and ceramic bowls filled with Halloween candy.

Some of the guests came wearing costumes and when Jay and her husband arrived, she announced that she'd decided to be a police officer for Halloween.

"So original," Juliet kidded her sister. "How did you ever think of it?"

Jack, dressed in a skeleton costume, ran the grill on the patio off the kitchen cooking kebobs and burgers and hot dogs. Friends from the resort stood around chatting and sipping drinks under the decorated pergola in Juliet's adjoining yard, and Justice moved happily from group to group soaking up the attention and enjoying pats and scratches behind the ears.

When it was time to eat, everyone squished around the small dining table or carried plates into the living room and took seats on the sofa and chairs to gobble up the grilled meats, chili, rice, cucumber and feta salad, and two kinds of soup, roasted cauliflower, and mushroom and potato.

After dinner, the friends got ready to walk into town and they left the house under Justice's supervision and the cat curled up comfortably in her soft rectangular bed in the corner of the living room and promptly fell asleep.

The group walked down the lane and turned right onto Main Street to join the streams of people heading for the common.

Approaching the movie theatre, a shiver ran though Shelly's stomach as she recalled the night Emma Pinkley hurtled her car around the corner and smashed into one the brick buildings.

Thinking about the murder, a wave of sadness washed over her.

Juliet noticed her friend's quiet demeanor, gave her arm a squeeze, and said, "I'm sure Emma is thankful for your help in solving the case."

"The dreams were pretty accurate," Shelly said. "I just had a hard time interpreting them."

"Are you starting to accept that the dreams are telling you something?" Juliet asked.

"Maybe. I don't know where they come from or how it could be possible that they try to point me in the right direction. But...."

"But what?"

"I like seeing my sister in the dreams." Shelly smiled. "It makes me feel that she hasn't left me."

Juliet nodded and teased, "Be sure to tell your sister not to leave me out of the dreams in the future."

"I think I know why you weren't in the dreams."

"Why wasn't I?" Juliet questioned.

Shelly explained, "Emma's true friends couldn't make the dinner that night. At least not until Peggy Lane showed up later. The people with Emma were her co-workers and acquaintances, not the women friends she really cared about. That's why you weren't with me in the dream. Best friends weren't around that night."

A smile crossed Juliet's face. "Okay then. I'll accept that explanation of why I was left out of it. But what did the money falling down from the ceiling have to do with anything?"

"I think those dollar bills represented Dawn's desire to get hold of the life insurance money on Emma. The money floated down to indicate possibility and rushed back up to represent Dawn's inability to get at it. Charlie would cash in the life policy, but he wasn't going to share it with Dawn."

"That makes sense. I think." Juliet's brow wrinkled in thought. "You can also tell your sister to stop being so mysterious with her clues in the dreams she sends you. How about just some straight up information next time?"

"I hope there isn't a next time," Shelly said.

Juliet gave her friend a skeptical look. "Right. You'd better enjoy tonight because the next mystery is most likely lurking around the corner."

When the friends reached the common, they headed for the row of games that had been set up along one side of the space. There was skee ball, and a basketball game, and darts, a short bowling lane, a pitching game, and a ball-rolling game to see if a player could get three balls to line up in a row.

Jack called to Shelly. "Let's see how we do on the bowling game." His eyes lit up like a little kid's.

Juliet and a few people from the resort bought cotton candy and went over to watch the others attempt the games.

Jack won a stuffed ladybug and presented it to Shelly with a kiss and a hug. "Do you know what the ladybug represents?"

Shelly shook her head.

Jack held Shelly's hand and pulled her close. "Well, some cultures believe that if you catch and release a ladybug, she will fly to your loved one's ear and whisper your name to her and then your true love will rush to your side." Jack took the stuffed animal from Shelly and gently put the ladybug's face near her ear. "See? What did she whisper to you?"

With a pink blush running up her cheeks, Shelly smiled at her boyfriend. "It's a secret."

The two walked hand-in-hand behind the group to find a spot on the hill where they could spread their blankets to watch the fireworks.

Jack said, "I know these cases are hard on you. Are you doing okay?"

"I guess so," Shelly told him. "It's hard to understand some of the awful things that happen in the world. It's hard to understand greed and hate ... lies, cheating ... the urge to kill. It can be so very disheartening."

"That's all true." Jack squeezed Shelly's hand in his. "But do you know what's uplifting? People who use their skills for good, to help, to make the world a better place, a kinder, more honest, and caring place. And you know what? I found someone like that right here in the little town of Paxton Park and she happens to be walking right next to me ... where I hope she'll stay for a long, long time."

Jack leaned down and touched his lips to Shelly's just as the first firework lit up the sky with orange and gold sparkles ... and a heart-shaking boom.

THANK YOU FOR READING!

To hear about new books and book sales, please sign up for my mailing list at:
www.jawhiting.com

Your email will never be sold, shared, or spammed.

If you enjoyed the book, please consider leaving a review. A few lines are all that's needed. It would be very much appreciated.

ALSO BY J.A. WHITING

OLIVIA MILLER MYSTERIES (not cozy)

SWEET COVE COZY MYSTERIES

LIN COFFIN COZY MYSTERIES

CLAIRE ROLLINS COZY MYSTERIES

PAXTON PARK COZY MYSTERIES

SEEING COLORS MYSTERIES

ABOUT THE AUTHOR

J.A. Whiting lives with her family in Massachusetts. Whiting loves reading and writing mystery and suspense stories.

Visit / follow me at:

www.jawhiting.com

www.bookbub.com/authors/j-a-whiting

www.amazon.com/author/jawhiting

www.facebook.com/jawhitingauthor

Printed in Great Britain
by Amazon